Eli swallowed hard as Mary called for the K-9 to come forward.

"Bullet, *volg.*"

Bullet obeyed, coming to heel next to Mary's left side. She scratched him under the chin. "Who's my good boy?"

That was apparently code for *at ease*, for the dog bounded forward, barking playfully. After a moment, he approached Eli. Eli stood perfectly still, waiting for the dog to—

What? Chomp his leg off? Go for his throat? He had to get over his nerves.

Like *yesterday.*

"Can I touch him?" Eli asked tentatively.

"Absolutely. He's yours, you know."

Eli reached forward, then paused. "Wait. What do you mean, he's *mine?*" Mental alarms pealed in his ears. "He belongs to the police department, right?"

"The department paid for him, yes."

"Good, then." For a moment he'd had the unnerving picture of having to take the dog home with him. "So now what?"

"Now we train."

"Train? I thought the dog already *was* trained."

"Oh, Bullet's trained," Mary replied, her chuckle softened by the kindness in her gaze. "I was talking about *you.*"

Books by Deb Kastner

Love Inspired

A Holiday Prayer
Daddy's Home
Black Hills Bride
The Forgiving Heart
A Daddy at Heart
A Perfect Match
The Christmas Groom
Hart's Harbor
Undercover Blessings
The Heart of a Man
A Wedding in Wyoming

His Texas Bride
The Marine's Baby
A Colorado Match
Phoebe's Groom
The Doctor's Secret Son
The Nanny's Twin Blessings
Meeting Mr. Right
†*The Soldier's Sweetheart*
†*Her Valentine Sheriff*

*Email Order Brides
†Serendipity Sweethearts

DEB KASTNER

lives and writes in colorful Colorado with the Front Range of the Rocky Mountains for inspiration. She loves writing for Love Inspired Books, where she can write about her two favorite things—faith and love. Her characters range from upbeat and humorous to (her favorite) dark and broody heroes. Her plots fall anywhere in between, from a playful romp to the deeply emotional. Deb's books have been twice nominated for the RT Reviewers' Choice Award for Best Book of the Year for Love Inspired. Deb and her husband share their home with their two youngest daughters. Deb is thrilled about the newest member of the family—her first granddaughter, Isabella. What fun to be a granny! Deb loves to hear from her readers. You can contact her by email at debwrtr@aol.com, or on her MySpace or Facebook pages.

Her Valentine Sheriff
Deb Kastner

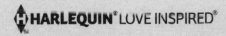

Recycling programs
for this product may
not exist in your area.

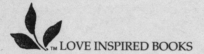 ™ LOVE INSPIRED BOOKS

ISBN-13: 978-0-373-81747-4

HER VALENTINE SHERIFF

www.Harlequin.com

Printed in U.S.A.

For I know the thoughts that I think toward you, says the Lord, thoughts of peace and not of evil, to give you a future and a hope.
—*Jeremiah* 29:11

To those who are lost, that God may find you, and that you may find Him. And to those whose path is shadowed, that He might give you light.

Chapter One

Serendipity, Texas, had gone to the dogs.

Literally.

Eli Bishop couldn't help but find *some* dark twist of humor in that irony—for him, anyway.

Despite the uneasiness skittering up his spine, he stood ramrod-straight with his shoulders set and his chin up, the last man of five comprising the straight line of the small-town police force. Anxiety clouded his chest as Captain Ian James elaborated on his new plan for a Serendipity police dog.

"Due to the recent influx of over-the-border drug trafficking, we've decided to incorporate a K-9 unit into the Serendipity Police Department," the captain announced, his hands clasped behind him and a stern set to his dark blond brow. He paced back and forth in front of the small squad of cops assembled before him, making eye contact with each one down the line.

"It is imperative that we stop these crimes before they become a threat to the peace and security of our town, and the best way to do that is to acquire a fully trained K-9 unit. I'm pleased to announce that, as of January 1, we've been funded for one of our own. We'll be using it both in police work and, as the need arises, in search and rescue to deal with increasing difficulties in weather situations through our county. I have been working in tandem with a national agency to select the best possible candidate among our officers to work with the K-9 in this program."

The hair on the back of Eli's neck stood at full alert as the captain stopped before him. Sweat beaded on his forehead.

This was irrational.

Unreasonable.

He was making a big deal out of nothing. He was stronger than the fear of dogs he'd carried with him since childhood. He *was*. But that didn't stop his shoulders from rippling with tension as he pulled in a long, calming breath through his nostrils and fisted his clammy palms tightly against his sides.

He couldn't let a stupid phobia wreck an opportunity for promotion. He had always been competitive and ambitious, whether it was playing football in high school or being first in his class at the police academy. With his personal life recently taking a serious nosedive, he was at the point where there was nothing he wanted quite so much as the opportunity to prove his mettle to the department. His career was all he had left, and he was game for almost anything, except—

Please, Lord. Not this.

Eli forced himself to remain motionless, his gaze steady but empty. Over the years he'd perfected the art of not showing what he was thinking. It had held him in good stead, until now. He wasn't sure he could mask these emotions.

"Bishop, you'll be pleased to hear that the honor is yours."

Eli tried to steady his breathing, but his throat closed around the air.

Pleased? This wasn't an honor. It was a horror. His own personal nightmare. He clenched his jaw in a vain attempt to control the tremor that ran through him.

He could handle bad guys. Knives. Guns. Whatever else was thrown at him, no matter how frightening. Even a broken engagement, as awful as that had been.

But dogs? That was another thing entirely.

Eli cleared his throat. "Sir, may I respectfully suggest—"

Captain James abruptly sliced the air with a clipped movement of his hand and shut Eli down midsentence.

"Perhaps I haven't made myself clear."

The captain's voice was in command mode, and Eli knew he'd already lost the battle. Probably even the war.

"This is a direct order. I have taken the liberty of vetting you for this training through the national organization I mentioned. Everything has been approved and arranged. Mary Travis is expecting you at her house at promptly fourteen hundred hours today to start working with your new partner. She's training the K-9 herself, and she's graciously agreed to help you adjust to your new role as handler."

Eli stifled a groan as the bad news kept piling on. He knew it would take more than a little *adjusting* for him to be able to work with a dog, especially an aggressive one. A K-9 would no doubt fall into that category. He definitely needed to bring his A game, if he wasn't going to come out looking like an idiot.

What was worse—far worse—was that Mary Travis probably already thought he was a moron with a capital *M*. After all, it was her sister, Natalie, who'd left Eli high and dry one week before their wedding. No explanation. No hint of what was to come, or that anything had even been wrong with their relationship.

Clearly something had been. He still didn't know what.

Mary probably knew more than he did—which was exactly why he didn't want to work with her.

He nearly choked on his own breath as tidal waves of humiliation washed over him. He would rather have been paired up with practically anyone else in town—anyone who hadn't had a front-row seat to the way Natalie had ditched and disgraced him. He was certain his ego would never be able to withstand the hit were Mary to discover he couldn't even handle himself around a dog.

"Sir, Mary's work as a large-animal vet has her in high demand," he pointed out. "I'm sure she's already overbooked as it is. Are you certain she is going to have time to—?"

"Ms. Travis," the captain barked, cutting Eli off midsentence, "is already on board for this project. Her assistant is taking over her veterinary practice, so she can focus on her training kennel full-time. She has certification in search and rescue, and is branching out to include training small-town police K-9 units. Her expertise in this project will be invaluable, and you *will* follow her instructions. Do we understand each other?"

Captain James stopped and faced Eli, nose to nose, with their gazes locked in unspoken combat. The sharp smell of wintergreen gum tickled Eli's nostrils. He bit the inside of his bottom lip, knowing that sneezing would definitely *not* be the response the captain was looking for. There was nothing to say that would change the decision, so despite the fact that his pulse was working overtime and his mind was screaming to the contrary, Eli remained silent.

The captain jerked his chin affirmatively and flashed Eli a satisfied smile. "Bishop, we'll talk promotion and benefits later. Company dismissed for lunch." Without another word, he turned on his heel and walked away.

The squad visibly relaxed, all except for Eli, who remained stiff at attention for several more seconds. He couldn't seem to break the hold the captain's words had on him. Red-hot electricity bolted down his spine, setting every nerve ending aflame. Adrenaline roared through him, and his fight-or-flight instinct burned in his veins the same way it did when he was in pursuit of a suspect.

Only this was worse, because he wanted to flee.

He had to cool off and get his head on

straight, if he was going to face the afternoon class with any form of dignity intact. Thankfully, after lunch and some paperwork, he had time for a quick ride on his motorcycle. His bike was his refuge—especially with the mild January wind in his hair and the freedom of the road with no one else around for miles. He did his best thinking and praying on the open stretches of land around the small town he called home.

Soon he was heading southbound on the road out of Serendipity, the reassuring purr of the motorcycle engine underneath him. He had a little less than an hour to wrap his mind around his new responsibilities before he had to present himself at Mary Travis's place, hopefully with a clear head and the fortitude he'd need to complete the task at hand. He revved the engine and sped down the highway, keenly aware that he was exceeding the posted limit. He was a cop, and he should know better, but there wasn't a car on the road for miles. It was a token protest against circumstances entirely beyond his control.

After about twenty minutes, Eli turned his bike back toward Serendipity, slowing his speed to match his own reticence, even as he reminded himself that there was no sense putting off the inevitable. Surely God had His reasons for this trial. It came with a promotion, for one thing.

And maybe, just maybe, it would take the heat off of Eli's personal life.

A tough guy with a dangerous dog. Who could beat that?

Maybe he'd no longer be known as the sap who'd been ditched almost at the altar. There had to be an upside, right?

He just hoped Mary Travis wouldn't be able to see through the thin veneer of courage he'd worked up during his ride.

He pulled his bike in front of Mary's light blue ranch-style house and removed his helmet, sweeping the sunglasses from his eyes. Mary's home stood on a fairly sizable plot of land— not enough for ranching or farming, but plenty of room for her kennels. He could already hear high, piercing yips and low, throaty barks coming from the vicinity of her front door, and his stomach gave an uncomfortable lurch that he sternly refused to call fear.

He paused for a moment outside the front door, swallowing hard and mindfully unclenching his fists. He'd forgotten to ask Captain James how long he anticipated this procedure would take.

One week, maybe?

Two?

Hopefully he could get in and get out without

much time and hassle. Accomplish his objective and move on.

Eli combed his fingers through his hair, slid his palm across his scratchy jaw and straightened his shoulders, unwilling to yield to the tightness in his chest. He knocked firmly, knowing he'd have to be heard over the raucous cacophony of wildly barking dogs.

Mary surprised him by answering right away, almost as if she'd been waiting for him. Maybe she had been, since they had an appointment scheduled. Hopefully she hadn't been watching him struggle from behind her front curtain. He shifted uncomfortably.

"Eli," she greeted with a warm but somewhat reserved smile. She straightened her black-rimmed glasses, calling attention to pretty green eyes. "Please come in."

Easier said than done, since the door was crowded with canines of various shapes, colors and sizes. He eyed the doorway but didn't move.

Mary merely laughed. "Or maybe I should have said, 'Welcome to the chaos.'"

Mary could see that Eli looked uncomfortable, probably something to do with the chaos she'd just mentioned. She pulled on the collar of her large black Lab, Sebastian, urging him out of the way. She used the other hand to point behind her, commanding the rest of the dogs surrounding her to move backward. In hindsight, she realized she should have penned them all in the den before Eli had arrived, but she hadn't thought about it. She was used to dogs milling around her and getting under her feet, but most people—Eli included, if the expression on his face was anything to go by—weren't accustomed to it.

He looked miserable, as if he would rather be anywhere but here—not that she could blame him for feeling that way. And *that,* she was certain, had nothing whatsoever to do with the dogs. Her chest tightened, and raw emotion scratched at her throat.

Great. So now she was about ready to burst into tears.

Real professional, Mary. Get a grip on it.

She straightened her glasses again and with them her spine, determined to do whatever must be done.

If it was anyone except Eli—but it was Eli. And this was a part of the process neither one of them could avoid. Since the moment she'd heard that Captain James had selected Eli for the K-9 unit, she'd been concerned about their working together. Eli had every reason for wanting to avoid being around her, and there was nothing she could do to make it easier for him.

Or her, for that matter.

And Eli was still standing on her front porch.

"Get back, Horace," she ordered, gently pushing a fluffy husky's hindquarters for emphasis. "Francis—off you go," she said to a Boston terrier with three legs. "And you, Sebastian," she said to the Labrador retriever whose collar she still held. "Back to the den. Shoo!"

Eli's striking blue eyes widened and his jaw went slack when the animals obeyed.

"What?" she asked hesitantly.

"I can't believe all those dogs did what you wanted them to do. It was almost as if they understood what you were saying to them."

Astonished and not a little bit perplexed, Mary shook her head. Hadn't Eli ever been around a dog before? Serendipity was a ranching community. Nearly every family in town had at least one working dog, a collie or a shepherd to help herd their stock. But Eli's amazement appeared to be genuine.

"Of course they did what they were told. They recognize the tone of my voice, if not the words. Dogs are smart animals. Even if they didn't exactly comprehend what I was telling them, they understand my hand gestures and body language. Weren't you around any dogs growing up?"

He stiffened and shifted his gaze away from her. "Nope."

She waited for him to elaborate. He didn't.

"Cat person?"

"Not so much."

"I see." She didn't. But what was she supposed to say? "Then this will be a new experience for you."

"Yep."

Enough with the clipped answers, already. She was sufficiently nervous to begin with, even without having to carry both ends of the conversation. Was this what it would be like to work with him over the next few weeks? Curt, almost brusque responses to every question she had for him?

His attitude confused her. She knew Eli to be friendly and kind, and right now he wasn't either. She took a deep breath and fervently prayed for guidance. And patience. It was apparent she was going to need healthy doses of both to get through the rest of this day. She stepped sideways, holding the screen door for Eli so he could maneuver around her and into the house.

He dragged his fingers through his thick black hair and eyed the doorway but didn't move to enter.

"Let's try this again, shall we?" she prompted. "Please, come in."

Eli stepped gingerly into the house and halted suddenly, raising his arms to shoulder level as a tan-colored whirlwind jumped out from behind the door, yipping up a storm, turning in tight circles and sniffing at Eli's ankles. The little apple-headed Chihuahua couldn't have been more than seven or eight pounds, but he was full of spit and vinegar, and she supposed he could appear a little startling to guests.

Once again Mary chided herself for not locking up the dogs before Eli arrived. His disdain for, or at the very least discomfort with, this whole situation was evident in every step he took and his closed expression. She watched helplessly as Eli braced himself, his shoulders squaring as he pressed his lips into a straight, firm line.

Mary reacted instinctively against the wave of anxiety and embarrassment that washed over her, hastily scooping the dog into her arm. She was angry at Natalie all over again for putting her in this position. Here within her own home, Mary stood, awkward and uncomfortable, when she should be completely in her element. Here with the dogs she fostered and trained, and her newly created Rapport Kennel. Here with Eli, a man she'd known since her youth and greatly admired.

No, it was not fair, and it was not right.

But thanks to Natalie, the situation was at best uncomfortable and at worst impossible. Not knowing what else to do, she held up the Chihuahua for Eli's inspection. "Behave yourself, young man."

Eli lifted a questioning brow.

Mary offered a confused smile and then burst into gentle laughter. "I was speaking to the Chihuahua," she clarified. "This little guy is Goliath. His bark is worse than his bite. It might sound like he's growling, but in truth he's just talking to you."

"Good to know. Snarls aren't a warning— they're a welcome." He tentatively reached a hand forward so Goliath could sniff his fingers. "On someone's planet, anyway," he rumbled under his breath. Mary thought he was speaking more to himself than to her, but she answered him anyway, choosing to make light of the comment, and not take it as an insult to her and her profession.

"Yep, that's my planet, all right." Mary was aiming toward cheerful, although she was fairly certain she'd missed the mark by a wide distance. "My world, filled with dogs of every size, shape and form."

The left side of Eli's jaw twitched. "Sounds like paradise."

Sarcastic much? He was about as enthusiastic about this new program as a chicken with his head on the chopping block, which left Mary to wonder, not for the first time, why he'd been chosen for the K-9 unit. Everyone in town, including Captain James, knew Eli had been jilted by Natalie. Surely it had occurred to him that the situation might lead to difficulties with the training. It had certainly occurred to *her;* though at the moment, she didn't have a clue what to do to make this an easier transition for Eli. Surely he had to realize that she couldn't help what her sister had done.

Maybe there wasn't anything she could do, except plow forward, right through the middle of Eli's morose attitude. She lifted Goliath to eye level and turned the dog so she was addressing his snout. "He's only six months old, so he's still learning his manners. Goliath, that is not how we treat guests in our home."

The Chihuahua yipped once and licked Mary's thumb.

Eli cleared his throat and rocked back on his heels, jamming one hand into the pocket of his blue uniform slacks.

"Captain James spoke to you?" he prodded,

scratching the back of his neck with his free hand, his dark hair curling around his fingers.

"About the new K-9 unit?" Mary nodded. "Oh, yes. I have to say, Ian is quite enthusiastic about the idea."

"Isn't he, though," Eli mumbled in agreement. He didn't sound happy about the prospect.

She decided not to acknowledge his lack of enthusiasm. Surely things would get better once he got to know his new partner.

"It's a great opportunity for you and for me, as well. I don't know how much you're aware of the work that I do here. I'm just now getting my training kennel off the ground. Your department is my first official K-9 program. My proving ground, so to speak."

"Meaning I'd better be on my best behavior."

His eyes lightened to sky-blue, and the strain around his mouth eased, lessening the gravity of his expression. When he looked like that, it was harder to ignore the fact that this was the man she'd had a secret, desperate crush on for so many years....

But that was in the past. She was years past being a silly teenager crushing on the hotshot high school football star. He was a client now—the most important client she'd ever had. She couldn't let herself lose sight of that just because he had the bluest eyes she'd ever seen.

"You'd better believe it. Are you ready to meet your new partner?" A lot of thought had gone into the pairing of dog to man and man to dog, and she was proud of what she'd accomplished. She couldn't wait for Eli to meet his new partner, and her eagerness bubbled over in her voice. She recognized that this was one of those defining life moments she'd look back on, either with delight or utter mortification. It was all on Eli to make that call. If he lightened up, this could be good—maybe even fun. Working with a K-9 was every bit as much about enthusiasm and reward as it was about effort and exertion. Perhaps more so.

"Sure. Whatever." He shrugged offhandedly, as if it didn't matter to him one way or the other whether or not he met his partner.

Mary sighed in exasperation. Even if he wasn't thrilled about working with her, she thought he'd display a bit more interest in his new dog. His cavalier attitude was going to have to change, or they would never be able to work together. Where was the man with the happy-go-lucky smile for the world? Who had replaced him with Mr. Chip-on-His-Shoulder? Was it just because of Natalie, or was something else entirely wrong here?

Mary hadn't a clue. And it wasn't as if she

could ask. How did one even broach a subject like this?

She paused and tilted her face up to his, her gaze lingering on him, questioning him without words. Rather than meeting her eyes, his gaze wandered to somewhere in the vicinity of her chin.

"Are you okay?" she asked.

"I don't know what you mean." It was an adamant denial, even though she hadn't accused him of anything. He gestured toward the den. "I'm trying to follow orders here. Please. Lead the way." There was an element of pleading in his tone that hadn't been there before.

He was giving off mixed signals all over the place—which he clearly wasn't going to acknowledge. And if he wouldn't, she couldn't.

"So we're good, then?" she asked.

"Yes, ma'am." His voice was low and gruff, and his gaze turned so dark that his stormy blue eyes took on an almost black hue to them.

She wasn't going to solve any of their problems this way. Maybe the best thing to do was to bring out the big guns—

—or more specifically, the *Bullet*.

Chapter Two

Eli's chest tightened almost painfully as he followed Mary through the front room and into the den. In his opinion, it was more of a kennel than a living space. There were several crates, the smaller stacked on the larger, but they were all empty. The dogs who'd greeted him at the door were lounging on fluffy pillows of various shapes, colors and sizes, all of which looked as if they had been haphazardly tossed around the room. Chew toys, ropes, tennis balls and rawhide bones littered the floor.

The whole place was messy. Lived-in. And distinctly feminine. Everything from Mary's choice of floral wallpaper to the soft pastel curtains screamed *woman,* unlike his own apartment, which was meticulously clean and simply furnished with only the bare necessities in mahogany and stainless steel. Not much in the way of decor, other than a couple of family pictures on the wall. Eli didn't require too many things to live comfortably.

Besides, he liked clean. Uncluttered. Mary apparently felt differently.

He didn't know what he'd expected the inside of Mary's house to look like, since he knew she shared her space with all her dogs. He supposed he hadn't really considered it at all.

In any respect, this wasn't it. These pups looked as if they were living the lives of royalty, not as if they were working animals. He surveyed the dogs. The Chihuahua wasn't a K-9, formidable attitude notwithstanding, but he supposed some of the other dogs could be.

In addition to those he'd seen in the front room, there were three other large canines—one a creamy yellow color but otherwise identical to Sebastian, a gray dog with whiskers and a lot of fluff on its legs and another that looked a little like Lassie from the old television show.

He wondered which of them would be his. To his relief, they were not overly intimidating. None of them seemed as if they could be a police-trained K-9, either, not that he really knew how to assess one.

"If you'll follow me to the back patio, I'll introduce you to your new partner. He's in the yard getting some exercise with some of the other pups."

"There are more?" The question was half tongue-in-cheek jesting and half utter bemusement. "How many dogs did you say you have again?"

Mary glanced back and smiled. "Too many. I've lost count."

Eli shook his head and chuckled. "I'm not surprised."

She stopped at the sliding glass doorway and turned to face him, gesturing back toward the den. "You've met Goliath," she said, pointing to the Chihuahua. "The gray one is a standard schnauzer—Periwinkle. I call her Perry." Upon hearing her name, the schnauzer pricked her ears. "And of course I have my SAR dog, Sebastian. He's a Labrador retriever, and he pretty much never leaves my side." She took a breath and smiled, making a sweeping gesture that encompassed both the den and the yard. "The rest of this sorry lot I'm either fostering or training."

"SAR?"

"Search and rescue," she elaborated.

"I see. And my dog?"

"Bullet. He's a Dutch shepherd. That's him right there," she said, aiming her finger to the far corner of the yard.

Eli's gaze shifted to where she'd pointed, his

shoulders tensing as he silently observed Bullet, a mostly black-furred dog with a bit of tan on his face and legs. He was trotting around the perimeter of the wooden security fence as if he were staking his claim on it. The dog circled a few of the obstacles in the yard—a balance beam, a chute and a couple of jumps—punctuating his sniffing with an occasional ominous bark.

Bullet was definitely more what Eli had imagined in a K-9, both in aggression and demeanor. Eli was pretty sure bad guys wouldn't want to run into the sharp-toothed end of this dog. *He* wouldn't.

He steadied his breath, trying not to think of another dog, another time, a terrifying episode that had resulted in permanent bite marks and gashes on his right forearm and shoulder. He had many scars on his body, everything from the sharp edges of an angry bull's horn across his ribs to the ragged pucker of a knife wound on his chin. Yet comparatively, those had been easier to heal, emotionally speaking. He didn't dwell on them.

Not like his inexplicable, irrational fear of dogs. Experts even had a scientific name for it—cynophobia—which didn't help him a bit. He couldn't get over it, no matter how hard he tried.

He swallowed hard, his muscles rigid as Mary called for the K-9 to come forward.

"Bullet, *volg.*"

Bullet obeyed the command immediately, coming to heel next to Mary's left side and sitting on his haunches, looking up at her expectantly for his next instruction. She reached down and scratched him under the chin. "Who's my good boy?"

That was apparently code for *at ease,* for the dog bounded forward, barking playfully. After a moment, he approached Eli, circling his legs and sniffing him. Eli stood perfectly still, staring down at the dog and waiting for him to—

What? Chomp his leg off? Go for his throat?

His imagination was getting the best of him, and it certainly wasn't helping him with this situation. He had to get over his nerves.

Like *yesterday.*

"Can I touch him?" Eli asked tentatively.

"Absolutely. He's yours, you know."

Eli reached forward, allowing Bullet to sniff at his fingers before he scratched the dog behind the ears.

"Good boy," he said to the dog, and then paused abruptly as Mary's words penetrated his muddled brain. "Wait. What do you mean, he's *mine?*" He straightened, mental alarms pealing in his ears. "He belongs to the police department, right?"

Mary's gaze widened, and her lips pursed,

accentuating her cheekbones. She must have realized he was staring at her, because she immediately dropped her gaze. Her heart-shaped face turned a pretty shade of rose.

"The department paid for him, yes," she answered after a tentative pause.

"Good, then." Relief washed through him. For a moment he'd had the unnerving picture of having to take the dog home to live with him. Thankfully that wasn't the case. "So now what?"

"Now we train." Mary straightened, resuming the professional demeanor with which she'd met him at the door. "Since it's Friday afternoon, I suggest we break for the weekend and pick this up first thing Monday morning."

"Train? I was given the impression that the dog already *was* trained," he said, cautiously running a palm down Bullet's neck. Eli jerked his hand back when Bullet raised his head. "Isn't he a certified K-9?"

"Oh, Bullet's trained," Mary replied, her chuckle softened by the kindness mingling with the amusement in her gaze. "I was talking about *you*."

Mary paced the front room, glancing out the window every few minutes, waiting for Eli to arrive for his first official training session with Bullet. It seemed as if the weekend had dragged on for a lifetime, but Monday morning had finally come, and Eli was due soon. They'd agreed on eight o'clock to start, and it was only half past seven, so it wasn't as if he was late. She was just anxious to see him again—to get started on the real training process. It was an exciting moment for her and for her newly established Rapport Kennel.

If nerves over her business weren't enough to make her antsy, she couldn't seem to be able to get Eli out of her mind. It bothered her more than she cared to admit—because if she were being honest, this wasn't all about work. It was about the man she was working with.

Eli. The man who for years had filled her dreams, as hopeless as they were. Mooning over a man who hardly knew she even walked the planet. But that was long ago, when she was an awkward teen. She'd been over him for years.

He was her past. Except now, he wasn't.

He was very, very present.

If she could have framed the expression on his face when she'd teased him about training *him* and not the dog, she would have hung it over her fireplace, where she could appreciate his handsome mug every time she walked by. Of course that might be a little problematic to explain to visitors, since it was none other than her very own sister who had jilted him for another man only a week before their wedding.

Not exactly the kind of picture a woman ought to place on the mantel, even in her mind and even in jest.

She was still angry at Natalie. At the moment, they weren't on speaking terms. It grated on her, knowing that in Natalie's tinted reality, Eli had been nothing more than the last in a long string of broken hearts. Her sister had always been a bit of a narcissist, but her selfishness had hit an all-time high with this one. Without a word of explanation to anyone, she'd left the state with a wealthy fellow the family had never even met. It was cruel, even for her.

How could Natalie have done such a thing? And to Eli, of all men? He deserved so much better than that.

He was a decent guy through and through. He didn't purposefully snub anyone, not even in high school, when he was the handsome and sought-after star running back on the football team. He went out of his way to make folks feel welcome—even going so far as to take pity on an awkward ninth-grade girl standing alone in a shadowed corner of her first Sweetheart Social.

He wouldn't remember that particular incident, of course.

But she did.

She'd never forgotten any of the kind things he'd done for her over the years. To be honest, if only with herself, she'd have to admit that her feelings for Eli had shaded every romantic relationship she'd had over the years. No other man could compare to him, or at least to the man she'd built Eli up to be in her mind. It wasn't fair to the men she'd dated, and it definitely wasn't going to make working with the man Eli was now any easier.

He could hardly live up to perfection, and that was pretty much what she'd made him out to be.

Past tense. That part of her life was over long ago. She was over this. She was over *him*. She had to be. Now more than ever. How else would she be able to endure working with him every day?

And she *was* going to work with him. It might have come as a complete shock to her when Captain James had arranged for the two of them to work together in the new K-9 unit, but she wasn't about to turn down the opportunity she'd been praying for. If she presented a competent K-9 unit to the Serendipity Police Department, she'd be able to use that reference to get other clients in surrounding small-town areas, places that might otherwise not be able to afford to train such units. It was her dream to run a full-time training kennel, and she found she couldn't give it up, not even to spare Eli the discomfort of having to work with his ex-fiancée's sister.

She sank into the plush forest-green easy chair in the corner of her living room and folded her legs, wrapping her arms around her ankles. Resting her forehead on her knees, she closed her eyes and offered her heart to God in prayer.

She didn't realize how much time had passed, but at eight o'clock precisely, Eli knocked rhythmically on the door, *shave and a haircut, two bits.*

She was ready, and she hoped he was equally prepared for his first real lesson with Bullet. He'd seemed a little aloof about the dog on Friday.

She opened the door and smiled in greeting, and he simply marched past her.

"Let's do this," he said over his shoulder, already halfway to the den.

No *Hello.*

No *Good morning.*

No *How was your weekend?*

Just a curt *Let's do this,* in a voice that, while not what she would term callous, was nevertheless, in Mary's opinion, a little rough around the edges. Or maybe she was being oversensitive, and he was ready to get down to business.

"Okay, then," she answered blithely, tamping down her own emotions. Eli was probably nervous. She decided to cut him a break—this one time. She passed him, heading through the den toward the backyard without glancing around to see if he followed.

She didn't have to. She felt his gaze drilling into her back and knew he was scowling. What was up with that? Had he fallen off the wrong side of the bed? Eaten soggy cereal for breakfast?

As she stepped outdoors, she paused a moment, enjoying the sight of Bullet playfully barking and chasing Periwinkle and Sebastian around the yard. The dogs always made her feel better.

Eli was still staring at her, waiting for—*something*. For his training to begin, she supposed.

"Bullet, *volg,*" she called crisply, bringing the dog to heel.

"Do I have to talk like that—in another language?" Eli asked, stepping beside her and crossing his arms over the wide expanse of his chest. "What is that, anyway? German?"

He was so close, and so big, that she had the impression he was invading her personal space. She wished it didn't rattle her, but it did.

"You're close. It's Dutch. And, yes, I'm going to be teaching you a few Dutch words. Bullet is trained to respond to the language, though he knows most commands in English, as well."

"It figures," Eli groused, his brows lowering over startlingly arctic-blue eyes. "Dutch language for a Dutch dog. Just what I need. My partner and I not only have communication problems, we don't even use the same language."

Mary chuckled and laid a hand on his arm. "Bullet isn't really Dutch, and that's not why we use the language. He was bred right here in Texas. The foreign words help us—and the dogs—stay in the zone."

He shrugged one shoulder and quirked his lips. "I thought I was done being forced to learn new languages when I graduated from high school."

"I promise it's not as painful as you're making it out to be. Only a few words and they're fairly easy to pick up. You'll have a good time working with Bullet. Before you know it, it'll feel like it's all fun and games for you—probably the best time you've ever had on the police force. K-9 is at least as exciting as guns and knives."

Eli scoffed and shook his head, and Mary raised her eyebrows. Frustration burned deep lines of aggravation in her chest.

Why was the man being so contrary today?

He was acting like a toddler who didn't want to eat his vegetables. It didn't add up for a man as normally well tempered as Eli Bishop to be so unreasonably grouchy—not without a good reason.

But what reason could he have? Something was certainly stuck up his craw. Was he that uncomfortable working with her?

She sighed inwardly. She wouldn't blame him if he was. She wasn't feeling entirely composed herself. But the two of them would have to find a way to overcome the awkwardness between them, or they'd never be able to see this project through to completion—and that had to happen. It *had* to happen.

Could she bring up the source of the uneasiness between them? Force the issue? Address the elephant in the room—the one by the name of Natalie?

She cringed. While it would probably be better to bring their issues out into the open, the truth was, she was a bona fide, full-fledged chicken—just hear her cluck! She could no more mention Eli's relationship with Natalie than she could make the Earth orbit backward around the sun.

"We'll start with some basic commands, and then we'll play a few games," she instructed, consciously shoving her own emotions to the side and hoping Eli would do the same. She would have plenty of time to mull over their issues later, when he wasn't around to pick up on it. "Use *volg* to bring him to heel on your left side."

"V-log." Eli stumbled over the word. Bullet cocked his head, clearly interested in the strange man, but he didn't respond to Eli's voice as he had with Mary's. That was to be expected. Eli had to learn to give the commands with authority, and Bullet had to learn to trust Eli. It would just take time.

Mary took two large steps backward, away from Eli, giving Bullet a subtle hint to focus on the man before him. "It's *volg*. Try it again."

"Volg," Eli commanded in a low, firm voice, fisting his hands as he spoke. Bullet circled around him and sat perfectly at his left heel. Eli glanced up, his surprised gaze meeting Mary's. A smile crossed his lips. "Now, that's better."

Her stomach fluttered and pride welled in her chest, though she wasn't certain whether it was from Eli's reaction or Bullet's successful training. "Sure. See? It's not so bad. You just have to practice the new words until they become second nature to you. Probably a lot like your job—working through the ranks, learning as you go."

"Yeah," he agreed soberly. "Working through the ranks."

After applying the heel command successfully several more times, Mary taught Eli the words for stay, come, sit and down. Bullet, of course, already knew the commands. Eli fumbled through the Dutch, but he was a quick learner, and clearly determined to make it work between him and his new partner, which was exhilarating for Mary to watch.

Yet even in their best moments, there was some silent but unsettling subtext within the interchange between the dog and the man. It wasn't anything so blatant that she could immediately pinpoint the problem and correct it, but the exchange wasn't as flowing and straightforward as it should have been. Mary couldn't quite put her finger on what was off about it, but something was wrong.

She took her cues from Bullet rather than Eli. The dog occasionally shied sideways, which was unlike the well-trained K-9. Bullet's skittishness suggested his handler was agitated, and Mary watched Eli closely, looking for signs of anxiety. His expression was sober and his jaw set in determination, but she didn't necessarily think that was cause for concern. Eli had always been a bit of a perfectionist. Clearly he wanted to be successful in his new endeavor.

There was nothing wrong with focus and resolve. But sometimes when Eli would mix up his commands, the dog didn't know how to respond and returned to Mary's side, which only served to set Eli's face into a deeper scowl and widen the distance between him and his new K-9 partner.

How was she going to get him to relax? He'd been so laid-back in high school. She remembered him as the guy who always had a smile on his face, and his nature had been easygoing and friendly. But that was only her teenage love-struck observation. Maybe that wasn't his true personality at all...at least, not anymore.

People grew up. Things changed. And she couldn't say it was the first time he hadn't met her expectations. When he'd become engaged to Natalie, Mary had assumed he'd join in their family life and culture, but that had never happened. Serendipity was a small town with country ways, and family was a big deal here. Yet it hadn't appeared to matter to Eli.

Maybe he wasn't the way she had imagined at all.

Maybe he was still bitter and frustrated from being jilted only one week before the wedding.

Maybe he didn't like this situation.

Maybe he didn't like *her*.

Whatever was behind his shady mood, if

he wanted this program to work, he'd have to get over it and put forth a little more proactive effort.

He'd—*they'd*—get a lot further if he would relax. Bullet wasn't going to respond to inconsistent or turbulent emotions. The dog needed regular praise and enthusiastic feedback or all of the training in the world meant nothing. Bullet wouldn't work unless he thought it was a game.

How to express that to Eli was another thing entirely. She'd trained plenty of dogs, but this was her first cop. She didn't know how best to proceed, but she was fairly certain Eli wouldn't respond to criticism, even if it was constructive.

She paused, examining her own thoughts and actions. Dumping all the training commands on him at once might not have been such a great idea. Just because she'd easily picked up Dutch didn't mean Eli was going to. He'd been a jock in high school and had been good at math. She couldn't recall his performance in English or in the Spanish class he'd taken.

What if learning a new language had proven difficult for him in the past? That would certainly explain a lot, perhaps even why he was resisting her every effort on his behalf. Her heart softened toward him. Maybe if she backed off instead of pushing him so hard, his relationship with Bullet would progress naturally. It was certainly worth a try.

"Let's take a break from all this hard work. Why don't you and Bullet play for a while," she suggested.

"Play?" He turned to her and crossed his arms, another defensive gesture that set Mary's teeth on edge. "What does that even mean? You make it sound like we're fifth graders on a swing set."

"Something like that." Mary pinched back a sharp retort, refusing to be thrown by his cranky attitude and determined to work through it. She'd have to show him how much fun it could be to work with Bullet. She leaned down and scooped up a simple white bath towel that had been rolled the long way and strung together with rubber bands.

Eli arched a brow. "A towel? Really?"

Dog training wasn't about expensive equipment and fancy gimmicks. Mary ignored him and waved the towel toward Bullet.

"Come on, boy," she encouraged in the high voice she instinctively used with animals and children. "Come and get it."

Eli observed her silently, his lips pressed, and his posture stiff, while she played tug-of-war with Bullet and then threw the towel across the lawn for the dog to retrieve.

"You want to give it a go?" Mary offered the towel to Eli but he didn't grab for it. Instead, he took a step backward and jammed his hands into the front pockets of his pants. His lips curled downward. He wasn't nearly so handsome when he frowned.

He shook his head. "If you're only going to play with him, I think I'll pass. It doesn't look that complicated. You go on ahead. I'll grab one of those lawn chairs over there and watch."

Now it was Mary's turn to frown. She was doing everything she could to encourage him. *What* was his problem?

"Eli, seriously. You are never going to bond with Bullet if you don't personally interact with him. You guys are supposed to be a team, a unit. Dogs have different personalities just like people do. You have to learn his quirks and characteristics, and he needs to get to know your idiosyncrasies, as well."

Eli scoffed under his breath, but loud enough for Mary to hear it. The man was thoroughly exasperating in every respect. He was certainly nothing like the guy she'd been putting on a pedestal all these years.

Maybe he never had been.

"Are you going to do this or not?" she demanded, at the end of her emotional rope and quickly losing patience.

"All right, already." He snatched the towel from her grasp and tossed it across the yard in a long, high arc. "Nag," he muttered crossly, under his breath.

"Somebody's got to be," she retorted, propping her fists against her hips. "Do you give Captain James this much grief?"

His eyes widened. "No, of course not. I—"

He paused. His frown deepened for a moment before he offered her a rueful smile. "You're right, of course. I'm acting like a class-A jerk, aren't I?"

His grin sent her stomach aflutter. "You said it, not me."

"I'll try to do better," he promised.

"I'm sure you'll be fine," she assured him, surprised at the intensity of the relief that washed through her. She hadn't realized how very much she didn't want to have to butt heads with Eli. She could only pray things would go better from here, now that he'd checked his attitude. She'd just known he'd be the kind of man willing to own up to his mistakes, and it was heartening to be proved right.

Bullet sat on his haunches directly in front of Eli, wagging his tail. Eli tentatively reached for the towel and removed it from Bullet's mouth. "Now, what did you say when you tossed this old rag for him?"

"*Apport.* It means fetch."

"Yeah. I figured."

"Actually here's a little bit of useless trivia. I named my business Rapport Kennel. It's a play on words."

"Clever," he said, displaying his admiration in both his voice and his gaze.

Mary couldn't help but smile. She liked seeing the kinder side of Eli. Finally she was seeing a glimpse of the man she believed would eventually make an outstanding representative of the K-9 unit for the Serendipity police force.

"And what words do you use to play tug-of-war?"

"Grrr," she said with a laugh. "Just wag the cloth in front of his nose. He'll take it from there."

For once, Eli did as he was instructed and didn't complain about it. "All right, fellow. Show me what you've got."

Bullet barked and leaped for the towel. Eli involuntarily snatched his hand back and the dog bounded off with his prize.

"Hey, now," he protested, rushing off after the dog. "Get back here. That's not fair. You caught me off guard."

Mary wasn't sure that the dog had caught him unaware. It looked more like he'd startled him—she wouldn't go so far as to call it fear, but she noted it on her clipboard nonetheless. She was probably being too conscientious, but this was her first time training a K-9 team. It had to be perfect. Better to be safe than sorry.

Bullet advanced and retreated playfully, eventually dropping the towel by Eli's feet so he could play, too. Eli didn't hesitate this time. He made a low rumble from deep in his chest and shook the towel at the dog. Soon the two were in a full-out tugging match, dashing up and down the lawn as man attempted to best the beast. Bullet was clearly enjoying the interchange, but Mary watched Eli carefully, uncertain about how he felt about the exercise. His expression, coupled with the firm set of his jaw, appeared more resolute than exuberant. But at least he was trying. She had to give him that.

She sighed softly, her gaze lingering on Eli. There was much to appreciate. He was a large man and firmly muscled, but he moved and turned with a fluid grace of a bird in flight. She couldn't help but admire the way his biceps strained against the short-sleeved material of his uniform shirt as he weaved and pulled, jumped and twisted. He was absolutely stunning to observe—from a purely objective point of view. What woman wouldn't notice?

Reluctantly she shifted her attention from Eli

in particular to the interchange between dog and man, noting on her clipboard both strengths and weaknesses in their movements as a team, points Mary would eventually need to address. For now it was enough just to watch. If she enjoyed the exchange a little too much, and if her eyes strayed a little too often to Eli, it was for her alone to know.

She inhaled deeply and strictly reprimanded herself. *Keep your mind on your work, girl, or you're headed for trouble.*

Eli wasn't here to have her gawk at him. If he should happen to glance over and catch her expression in an unguarded moment, that would be the end of their association for sure, and she would lose the best chance she had to make her goal of running a training kennel a reality. Her dreams were worth too much for her to lose on something as silly as being caught gaping at an attractive man—even Eli.

Especially Eli.

Bullet vaulted around the man, anticipating Eli's moves with Bullet's own clever efforts. They were testing one another, each trying to best the other, and Mary couldn't help but smile indulgently. She could give herself a pat on the back for a job well done. They were getting to know and figuring out each other. Strengths and weaknesses, just as she'd instructed Eli to do.

The two were well matched. Mary had known they would be. Eli wasn't aware of it, but she'd chosen this dog specifically for him. And vice versa. They'd make a good team one day, when their training was done.

"Here's his favorite toy," Mary called, lofting a tennis ball at Eli, who caught it with ease. "Give it a toss and check out his response time. He's amazingly fast for his size."

Eli drew his hand back and threw the tennis ball in a high arc, whooping when Bullet dashed off after it. "Look at that dog run. No wonder you named him Bullet."

Pride welled up in her throat, and she smiled. "You got that, did you? Trust me, it'll come in handy when you're taking down a bad guy."

"Only the bad guys, though, right?" he asked. His tone was light but his gaze not so much.

"Of course. Bullet knows which side of the fence he's working."

Eli made a show of wiping the sweat from his brow in relief. "You have no idea how glad I am to hear that."

He sounded like he was teasing, but Mary sensed a serious undercurrent. "I assure you—once you've spent some time with Bullet, you'll find he's totally trustworthy. He'll have your back better than any partner you've ever had."

He raised a brow. Somehow he didn't look convinced, even when Bullet brought the ball back to him, sitting before him and lifting his head, offering the tennis ball to him.

"What do I do now?"

"Take the ball and throw it again. And again. And again. Bullet never gets tired of playing with his ball. That's what makes him so easy to train. He has a strong, almost obsessive drive."

"If you say so." He didn't sound like he believed her, and once again, Mary came to the conclusion that he was one of those men who had to see to believe, like the apostle Thomas with the wounds of Jesus.

It took all types, she supposed, though it would be a great deal less of a hassle for her if she didn't have to prove every little point to him. She would, though, even if Eli dragged his feet each step of the way. His reluctance made her all the more determined to find success with the K-9 team.

After several minutes of tossing the ball for Bullet, Eli pulled up to Mary's side, his eyes bright and his chest heaving with effort.

"What's wrong?" she queried when he hovered next to her, an expectant look in his eyes. "Has Bullet worn you out already?"

She realized as soon as the words left her lips that she'd said the wrong thing.

Again.

The brief hint of diversion and elation in his eyes disappeared as his lips curled downward and his brows lowered.

"Don't you think we should stop goofing around and get back to work?" His voice grated on her last nerve.

She felt as if he were judging her, accusing her of wasting his time. Like he knew better than she did what they ought to be doing as part of their training. And right when she'd thought they were starting to make a little bit of progress. The man ran as hot and cold as a faucet. Any semblance of composure she'd regained watching him play with Bullet cracked like a baseball through a glass window.

She knew exactly what she was doing, and she *wasn't* wasting time, despite what Eli might have to say on the matter. She forced a chuckle she didn't feel and met his gaze in an undeniable challenge. "That *was* work."

"Come again?"

"I said—" she began, but he cut her off midsentence.

"I know you're trying to take it easy on me with all of this *playing with the dog* stuff. You don't need to do that. Don't water it down for me. I'm ready to give those Dutch commands another go."

Water it down for him? So much for a teachable moment. At least the dog didn't interrupt when she spoke—or question her every instruction.

"I see." She stared at him, taking his measure. Something wasn't adding up. She sent up a silent prayer for guidance, wishing she could put her finger on what that *something* was.

"What?" he asked, sounding mildly annoyed. He shifted his weight onto the balls of his feet, as if he was getting ready to pounce.

Mary noted the movement and shook her head. "I think we've done enough obedience training for one day. There's a lot more for you to learn. I have something else in mind for you right now."

Eli groaned. "Don't tell me there's paperwork." He shook his head. "No, don't answer that. Of course there's paperwork. I'm a cop, and I'm still on the clock."

"No paperwork. Not today, anyway."

"Whew. Glad to hear it. Paperwork is the least favorite part of my job. I like to be up and active." He stretched side to side as if getting ready for a run.

"Then this next activity will be perfect for you."

"Yeah? What am I doing?"

"You, plural," she reminded him. "You're a

unit now. I assure you there will be plenty of movement involved—for both of you. I want you to run through a confidence course."

Chapter Three

A *confidence* course?

What was that supposed to mean? It felt like a personal dig, right into his rib cage. Was his lack of assurance so obvious that she felt the need to fix it? Was he wearing a flag on his back?

Great. It was only day one of training, and he was already failing miserably at his new assignment. She'd already figured him out, even if she was too kind to admit as much. How was he going to prove himself to her after this, never mind the whole department? Indignity chewed at his gut.

"What's a confidence course?" He squared his shoulders and lowered his eyebrows, blockading his emotions behind steel doors in the furthest recesses of his heart. All he could do now was redouble his efforts to appear impervious to his circumstances and completely at ease with his dog.

"Loosen up," she murmured, her voice rich and reassuring.

As if he could relax.

Another emotional jab, this time a direct uppercut to the jaw. She certainly had his number.

"Nothing to get stressed about. I just want you to run Bullet through some of these obstacles here." She gestured toward the agility stations positioned across the lawn. "We won't do all of them. Just enough for you to get your feet wet."

"Right. Then it's an obstacle course." Many of the hurdles looked like the ones he'd faced when he was at the police academy. He'd excelled there, first in his class. Physically and mentally, he'd conquered the course and bested his fellow officers with ease. It had seemed so simple back then. All he had to do was let his aggressive nature take over, and he'd blown the competition away.

He wasn't so sure he was going to do as well on this one. He could only speak for himself and not for his barking teammate. And he wasn't the least interested in unleashing Bullet's aggressive nature.

No, thank you.

That, he supposed, was the crux of the problem. He was used to fending for himself. Now he'd been thrown into a situation where he had to work as a team. It didn't help that his partner was an uncompromising canine.

"Let's not call it an obstacle course," Mary suggested, stroking her finger down the perfect little dimple in her chin. "I don't want you to think of the stations that way. Bullet will sense it, if you tense up, so I want you to let loose and have fun with it."

"Have fun with it," he repeated blandly. Yeah, like that was going to happen anytime soon.

"I prefer to think of the stations as challenges. It's mostly a team-building exercise, if you will, as you learn to navigate the course together. You're the unit leader, so it's up to you to set the pace. Snap the lead on to his collar and let's get started," she continued, handing him a six-foot leather leash.

"Which one do you want me to do first?" He attached the lead, gaining Bullet's immediate attention. Now would be a good time for him to prove himself. He only wished he felt more certain of his success.

"Let's go with the low hurdle right there. Set yourself at an easy jog and—"

Eli didn't let her finish. He bolted into motion with Bullet at his heel. When he reached the hurdle, he leaped over it with ease, expecting the dog to follow. Instead, Bullet sidestepped and ran around the jump, then turned in a circle around Eli, twisting him into a knot with the leash.

Making him look like an utter fool. Thank you, muttinski.

Thoroughly exasperated, he spun around on his heels, trying to extricate himself from the six feet of leather cord. It was all he could do to stay upright, and the last thing he needed was to face-plant himself in the dirt right in front of Mary. He imagined she was probably laughing at him already.

"You almost had it right," she said, reaching down to untangle the leash from Eli's ankles. She didn't appear to have found his distress amusing. He wanted to hug her. "There was only one minor detail you might want to work on."

"Only one?" Eli snorted. He'd already made enough mistakes to fill an entire stack of Mary's clipboards. "And that would be?"

"Well," Mary said, pursing her lips and then breaking into a smile. "Theoretically Bullet is the one who is supposed to navigate the hurdle. You're there for moral support. It was a nice jump, though. I'd give you a nine out of ten for technique."

He ought to be—expected to be—embarrassed at her teasing and laughter, but, for some unknown reason, she had put him at ease. Maybe it was the kindness in her eyes or the sweetness of her smile, but even though there was no doubt she was poking fun at him, he didn't feel like she was mocking him. Instead, he was pleasantly surprised to realize she was having fun *with* him, making light and joy of what would otherwise have been painfully awkward.

After being utterly humiliated by Natalie, Eli didn't trust women as far as he could throw them. But Mary was different. With her, what you saw was what you got. No games. It would have been enough for him to relax and feel comfortable around her—if it weren't for the dogs.

"You want me to give it another go?" He quirked his lips upward to show he was still in the running.

She smiled back at him and nodded, waving a hand toward the hurdle.

"All right, buddy, let's show the pretty lady how a K-9 jumps." He jogged toward the hurdle with Bullet on his left, and then dodged to the side as they approached the station. He wasn't giving the dog anywhere else to go but over, and he expected Bullet would have no problem complying. He was a large, energetic dog, and the jump was a small one. How hard could this be?

His plan was working well, all the way to the last moment, when Bullet pulled up and sat firmly on his haunches. Eli barely had time to react, changing direction just before the leash became taut. He didn't want to choke the dog, but he didn't want to land in an inglorious heap, either.

"Come on, big guy. Over the hurdle." He yanked gently on the lead, but Bullet obstinately fought him, wagging his head back and forth, and resisting the pressure Eli put on him. Eli wanted to throw up his hands in defeat.

That wasn't going to happen.

"You're embarrassing me, here, dude," he whispered to the dog. He swiped his palm across the stubble on his jaw, turned toward Mary and cleared his throat. "What am I doing wrong?"

"It's all about enthusiasm. Bullet's being stubborn to test you, to see how much you're going to let him get away with."

"So I need to be stricter with him?"

"The opposite, actually. Show him how excited you are to have him go over the hurdle, and he'll gladly cooperate with you."

"Excitement," Eli repeated in a less-than-enthusiastic tone. He scratched the back of his neck. This was more complicated than he'd imagined it would be. Mary made it sound like he needed to appeal to the dog's emotions. He couldn't even begin to comprehend such a thing. "Like how, exactly?"

Mary stepped forward and took the lead from Eli's slack fingers. She patiently walked the dog in a circle and straightened him out toward the jump.

"Come on, Bullet," she said in an overly energetic, saccharine-sweet falsetto. "Let's jump. Jump for me, Bullet. Come on. Come on, boy. You can do it."

It seemed like an awful lot of words for a single command, but Eli had to admit it worked. Bullet bounded forward and sailed over the hurdle with a foot to spare, then eagerly sat in front of Mary, waiting for her praise, which she gave in abundance.

"Your turn," Mary said, returning the dog to Eli. "Just remember to make it fun for him, and he'll do whatever you want him to do. It's not work for Bullet. It's a game. And be sure to give him lots of praise when he gets things right."

Eli gnawed the inside of his bottom lip thoughtfully.

"Fun. Right. All right. Bullet, jump." He nudged on the dog's lead and Bullet bounded forward, looking as if he were going to clear the hurdle with ease, as he'd done with Mary. At the last moment he once more turned, darting around Eli and leaving him yet again entangled in the six-foot leash.

Eli groaned. "I'm never going to get the hang of this," he muttered under his breath. He twisted, trying to release himself from the leather and only succeeding to make things worse.

"Sure you are. Let's get you out of these knots first, and then I want you to go stand right in front of the hurdle that's troubling you. I think the running start is giving him too much time to consider his alternatives."

Bullet hadn't *considered his alternatives* when Mary had put him over the jump. So why was it so difficult for Eli to communicate with the K-9? It seemed to him it wasn't the hurdle that was troubling him, it was the dog.

With Mary's help Eli got the lead untangled from his ankles. He took a deep breath and tried again.

"Volg," he commanded Bullet in a low, serious tone. The dog instantly responded, his attention completely on Eli as he walked toward the hurdle.

"Now put him in a sit-stay and step to the side of the jump, loosely holding the lead in your hand."

Eli commanded the dog to sit and stay using the Dutch words he'd been taught earlier in the day. To his surprise, Bullet responded to his voice.

"Good for you!" Mary praised. "I'm impressed. You remembered all of the foreign words. It took me a week to get them right."

Her praise was unexpectedly sincere, and Eli felt his ego crank up a notch or two. Not that she really had anything to be impressed about, but her kindness only made his resolve to prove himself quicken in his chest. He doubted she'd really had as much trouble learning the Dutch words as she was saying, but that only strengthened the impact of her words. Yet he was grateful she was giving him the opportunity to succeed.

"Remember, the more enthusiastic you are, the better Bullet will respond."

Eli moved to the far side of the hurdle, taking the slack from the lead and clicking his tongue. "Come, Bullet. Over."

Mary's laughter fluttered across the air between them. "You call that enthusiasm? Where's your animation? That sad excuse for excitement wouldn't motivate me to jump over any hurdles."

He wasn't trying to get *her* to jump. Anyway, it was impossible for him to rustle up any kind of real excitement. He'd been dreading every moment of this day from start to finish.

Of course, he'd gone out of his way to make sure she didn't know that, so he supposed he'd better start showing some of that *animation* she was talking about.

"Um—good boy," he said, his voice low and even. "Good boy, Bullet."

Mary propped her hands on her hips. "If that is the best you can do, we are in real trouble. Try using the voice you use when you talk to babies."

His gaze widened on her. "Babies? I don't usually talk to babies…ever."

"That's right. You don't have any nieces or nephews yet, do you?"

Eli couldn't help but chuckle at the thought of his sister, Vee, with a baby. She and her husband, Ben, were a couple of adrenaline junkies who were married to their fire department careers and the stateside mission ministry they were both involved in. And his older brother, Cole, was still serving in the navy. "I think it's safe to say that it is going to be a while."

"Try it anyway," she encouraged. "High, soft voice."

"Good boy," he repeated. He was aiming for a higher tone, but his voice was naturally low. Could he help it if he sang bass in the church choir?

Mary wrinkled her pert little nose at him. "Would that boring monotone motivate you?"

"I guess not." Mary could be stricter than a drill sergeant, even if she was a lot prettier to look at. He cleared his throat and tried again.

"Good boy!" This time his voice came out high and a little bit squeaky. It was embarrassing, really. Thank goodness none of the guys were around to hear it.

Mary let out a whoop. "That's it. Do it again."

He led Bullet the opposite way over the hurdle. The dog easily cleared the jump and turned toward Eli, wagging his tail. "Good boy. Good boy! Who's my good boy?"

Oh, the depths to which he had sunk.

Mary clapped in delight. "You've got it. I knew you had it in you."

To bounce around like an overactive toddler, talking in falsetto? He certainly never would have guessed he had that *in him* anywhere. Nor, up until this moment, had he ever wanted there to be. But if he could get the dog to do what he was supposed to do and please Mary in the process, so be it.

"Let's move on," she suggested. "Next up is the supported balance beam." She led him to a plank of wood that was about a foot wide and six feet long, propped up by a couple of old sawhorses that looked as if they'd seen better days.

"How do I get him up there?" Eli asked, eyeing Bullet. There were open stairs on either side of the sawhorses, but Eli wasn't sure how Bullet would respond to climbing a rickety old set of steps.

"The same way you did with the hurdle. Guide him with the lead. Then once he's up on the beam, you'll want to support him until he gains confidence."

"Support him how?"

"Put your arms around his middle. Give him enough room to move, but let him know you're there to catch him if he falls."

Eli swallowed the rising wave of panic that billowed into his throat. Just the idea of embracing a dog around his middle made the hair stand up on his neck. Nerves turned his stomach to mush. That Bullet had been trained by Mary only marginally lessened the dread pulsating through his veins.

He led Bullet to the stairs, half expecting the dog to balk as he had with the hurdle, but apparently Eli had established at least the semblance of authority, for Bullet climbed the stairs on the first try. Eli thought the dog looked stable enough as Bullet stepped out onto the plank. Eli kept one hand close to Bullet's flank and urged him farther out onto the beam.

"This first time, I'd really like it if you'd keep both arms around the dog." Mary's voice was firm, an order and not a suggestion.

"Hasn't Bullet done this before?"

"Yes, but not with you. If he should fall off the beam under your guidance, it will be that much harder for you to convince him of your leadership abilities, much less get him back up there again."

"Like a kid learning how to ride a horse."

"Yes. That's it, exactly. You're Bullet's partner. You want him to trust you implicitly, as much as you trust him to have your back in a dangerous situation."

Which would be exactly 0 percent. If only she had any inkling of how very skeptical he was of the canine species. He had to admit that Bullet seemed obedient enough, but he couldn't help that niggling bit of doubt that it would take only one frightening split second for the dog to turn and bare those sharp teeth on him.

With an entire lifetime of emotional resistance hindering him, it took every bit of strong will and self-control for him to wrap his arms around Bullet. Mary standing there tapping her pencil against her efficient little clipboard was the only thing that kept him in the game at all. He clenched his jaw and heaved air into his chest as he guided the dog across the beam, only releasing his breath when the dog trotted amiably down the back set of steps.

"Good job," Mary said, writing something on

the graphed page on her clipboard. "You only forgot one thing."

"What now?" Eli shook his head, his frustration mounting. She had no idea that he'd just gone against every self-protective instinct in his body to complete the mission she'd given him. "He crossed the plank and I didn't let him fall down."

"Praise, praise, praise," she reminded him in the high voice she used with the dog. "Don't ever forget to make this a happy time for the dog."

Eli wanted to roll his eyes. Happy time for the dog. Good grief.

"You want me to do it again?"

Mary glanced at her watch. "No, I think we're almost done for the day."

Relief washed through him that they'd finished the torture course, until his mind zoned in on one word. "Almost?"

"There is one last activity I'd like you and Bullet to complete together. Not paperwork, I promise." She nodded toward the house. "After you."

He swept a hand toward the patio, wondering what kind of new torment he was in for now. "Ladies first."

Eli followed Mary inside, more conscious of the dog trailing at his heel than he cared to admit. Mary displayed such effortless, fearless grace around her animals. What would she think of him if she discovered it had taken every last ounce of his courage to get through today's activities? He'd rather have been on the receiving end of gunfire. But at least he'd successfully worked through his first lesson, and that was saying something.

It would get easier. Wouldn't it?

"You mentioned one last activity?" His nerves crackled down his spine, and his fingers twitched into balled fists. Bullet had noticed, if not Mary. The dog kept nosing at his left palm.

"The same thing I imagine you do after exercising," she offered over her shoulder. "He needs to get cleaned up."

Eli skidded to a halt. Bullet circled him once and then sat down in front of him, peering up expectantly, waiting for a command.

Like what? *Shower?*

No way was he giving a seventy-five-pound bundle of fur and razor-sharp teeth a bath. He suddenly wished he was in Houston or Dallas and not in the tiny town of Serendipity. There were no groomers in town that he knew of. Otherwise he'd drop the dog off with a professional and pick him up when he was clean.

Of course he had the sneaking suspicion Mary wouldn't let him off the hook that easily, even if the option were available. She turned to face him, her hands propped on her hips. She'd been doing that a lot today. It felt like a reprimand. Eli stiffened.

"I'm going to ask you outright. How do you feel about the dog? Do you think you are well matched as partners?" Her green-eyed gaze met his and she tilted her chin with a stubbornness that surprised him. She was *challenging* him. Did she suspect the truth? "Don't you agree that Bullet will be more than sufficient for your purposes?"

"He's okay, I guess." Without lowering his gaze, Eli reached forward and scratched Bullet behind the ears. *Never let the enemy see your fear.*

Not that Mary was an enemy, though at the moment she felt mighty close to one.

"You *guess?* Bullet cost the department quite a tidy sum of money. He's been specially bred, and I trained him myself. All he needs is a good handler. You'd better be certain you are going to be that man, or I may be forced to request someone else for the job."

If he was going to back out, this was the moment. She'd left that door wide open and was practically goading him through it. Had she seen through the thin veil of his facade?

A part of him wanted to run for safety and

not look back. But Eli wasn't the kind of man to retreat from a challenge, even if this was the hardest trial he'd ever had to face. He'd experienced enough failure recently to last a lifetime. He couldn't afford to make any more mistakes. He had something to prove to himself—and to the men he worked with.

No excuses.

Nope. Not gonna happen.

"You don't have to do that," he countered firmly, pressing his lips to keep the quiver out of his voice. She wasn't the only one who could be determined. "You have my word. I'll do whatever it takes."

And he would. He would never have chosen this job of his own accord, but it *was* a promotion, not to mention the opportunity he'd been waiting for to redeem his value to himself and the world, to prove he wasn't a loser. He wasn't about to allow Mary to hand it off to another man.

She observed him silently for a moment before speaking. He felt like a fish in a bowl, and he struggled not to twitch.

Finally, after what felt like ages, she adjusted the rim of her glasses and nodded. "Okay. Let's go, then. I keep the tub in the mudroom."

Eli followed her, feeling like he should say something more to dig out of the hole he'd shoveled himself into, but what was there to say? He couldn't tell her why he was so reluctant to work with Bullet. He had to prove he *was* as enthused about the program as she and Captain James believed he should be, and that he was the right man for the job.

Tough and invulnerable. That's what he wanted them to see. That's what he wanted to *be,* although he expected that would be a long time in coming. As the saying went, just fake it till you make it, right?

He followed Mary to her laundry room, which was little more than a partitioned area off the kitchen. Clothes littered a large table between the washer and dryer. Some of the garments were stacked into loose piles, but mostly it was a haphazard mix of blouses and jeans. To the right side was a freestanding rack which contained more than a dozen empty wire hangers and no clean clothes.

"Sorry," she apologized briskly. "You caught me on my laundry day. As you can see, I managed to get most everything washed this morning, but hanging and folding, not so much." She smiled brightly, clearly not bothered by the clutter.

Eli didn't have a washer and dryer in his apartment, so he still brought his laundry home to his folks' house to use their machines. When he returned his starched, ironed clothes to his house, they were carefully placed into perfectly organized piles in his drawers and into his closet between color-coded dividers. His sister, Vee, often teased him about being a neat freak, borderline OCD, which he supposed was true to some extent. Otherwise he probably wouldn't have noticed the disarray that was Mary's laundry room.

Not his business. He had enough to worry about with this whole *washing the dog* business.

She gestured toward a large oblong steel tub in the back corner. A sprayer was affixed to the water pipes on one end. "Here we go, then. We'll put him in here and get him washed behind the ears and scrubbed under the paws."

Eli glanced down at Bullet, wondering how she planned to get the big dog into the tub, much less keep him there. As for washing the dog behind the ears, or anywhere else for that matter… Eli couldn't even begin to imagine, although the dark knot in the pit of his gut told him he was about to find out.

"Do you want to give Bullet a hand into the tub?" she asked.

Not especially.

He hesitated a moment too long to respond. He didn't know if Mary noticed his delay or if she was just in a hurry, but she didn't wait for him to act.

"Hop in, Bullet," Mary encouraged, tapping her palm against the inside of the tub, creating a tinny reverberation in the room. "Let's get you cleaned up."

Eli breathed a sigh of relief when Bullet bounded into the makeshift bathtub of his own accord. Maybe this wouldn't be so bad, after all.

Mary kneeled beside the bath. "Come down here beside me, Eli, and I'll show you how I usually soap him up. He's obviously a big dog with a lot of fur, so it takes quite a bit of shampoo to give him a thorough washing."

He knelt beside Mary and leaned his forearms against the rim of the tub. Bullet nudged him and he scratched the dog on the ear. "Does he like water?"

"He doesn't hate it. He's not as enthusiastic about getting wet as my Labs are, but I think he enjoys the end result. Wait until you see him preen when he's clean. He knows what a beautiful dog he is."

Eli took a mental step backward and tried to assess Bullet through Mary's shrewd eyes and open heart, but it was difficult, if not impossible, for him to perceive anything resembling beauty in a canine. Even his new partner couldn't break the mold of terror that lined the thoughts in his mind. All he could see was fur and fangs.

"Hand me the sprayer, please," she said.

He unhooked the apparatus and passed it over. "Should I turn on the water for you?" It was a not-so-innocent question purposefully asked with the slightest emphasis on the last two words.

Either she didn't notice or chose to ignore him. Instead, she demonstrated how the switch on the sprayer worked. "I have control of the stream from here. It's actually made for toddlers, but I've found it works wonderfully for my dogs. On. Off. Hot. Cold. Light spray. Heavy-duty stream. Pretty much whatever you need to get the job done."

"And here I thought all dogs were washed with garden hoses," he muttered under his breath. Not that he'd want to do that, either.

She chuckled in response. "Well, sure, in the summertime, but you wouldn't want a cold bath in the middle of winter, would you?"

"I guess not."

She switched on the spray and tested the temperature on her wrist, then soaked Bullet from head to toe. He expected the dog to object, but Bullet bore the stream of water with patience, only shaking his head once when Mary sprayed around his ears.

"Now we soap him up," Mary instructed, pointing to a pump bottle next to Eli's knee. "You want to do it?"

"Sure," he replied, refusing to give in to hesitation. It was time to step up, before Mary became suspicious and started questioning his motives and intentions again. He pumped a silver-dollar-size dollop of shampoo onto his hand and rubbed it into the fur on Bullet's back. The dog leaned into his touch, as if he was enjoying it. To Bullet it must feel like a canine massage, Eli supposed. Not so bad.

When he'd soaped the dog all over, Mary handed him the sprayer. He toggled the lever as he'd seen Mary do and then aimed the showerhead toward Bullet.

Unlike when Mary had wet him down, the dog didn't seem at all happy with Eli's attempt. He wriggled this way and that, making it nearly impossible for Eli to do a thorough job removing the soap from Bullet's fur.

"What am I doing wrong?"

Mary shrugged and shook her head. "I don't think it's you. He's just getting antsy. Maybe if you—"

The shrill chime of her cell phone interrupted the end of her sentence. She pulled the phone from the back pocket of her jeans and checked the number.

"I've got to take this. It's Samantha. I'll only be a moment," she said, holding up her index finger.

She was leaving him alone to rinse off a soapy wet dog?

"No, no, no, no, no," he exclaimed, half to Mary and half to Bullet, who wound himself around to see where Mary had gone. It was probably Eli's imagination, but he was almost certain Bullet looked at him with mischief in his eyes. Unorthodox panic leaped into his throat.

A dog wouldn't act up on purpose.

Would he?

The moment Mary stepped out of the room, Bullet whined, bunched himself up and shook for all he was worth. Eli crossed his forearms over his face and fell backward with a shout. That brief moment was all it took for the dog to take it into his mind to break free of his soapy bondage. Barking wildly, Bullet leaped from the tub and sprinted off toward the kitchen, his wet paws slip-sliding against the tile.

Eli caught his breath and exclaimed in shock. It wasn't only the dog's reaction that had caught him by surprise. The water Bullet shook onto him was a great deal colder than he'd anticipated.

Freezing, in point of fact.

No wonder Bullet hadn't been happy when Eli had tried to rinse him off. He hadn't remembered to check the temperature of the water on his wrist as Mary had done. Even though he didn't particularly like Bullet, he felt bad about the arctic dip. *He* most certainly wouldn't have liked to have been doused with ice water.

No, wait a minute. He had been. Bullet had gotten his revenge. Eli was soaked to the skin and shivering from the cold, with no conceivable way to regain his dignity.

Could this day get any worse?

"How's day one of training going for you? Is it everything you expected and then some?" Samantha Howell was one of Mary's closest friends, which also made her one of the few people who understood how important this new undertaking was to her. Her enthusiasm for the project showed in her voice. Samantha had recently had to fight her own battle to make her business dream a reality, so Mary felt a special kinship with her as she moved forward with Rapport Kennel.

Mary slipped out the back door and onto the porch where she wouldn't accidentally be overheard by Eli. "It's been good."

"You cannot possibly believe that pat answer

is going to work for me," Samantha chided. "I want details!"

Mary chuckled. No—her friend would not rest until she'd heard every last tidbit of information.

"It's been...challenging," Mary amended.

"Bullet giving you trouble?"

Air hissed between Mary's teeth as she held back a chuckle. "No. I wish it were that easy. I'd know what to do with Bullet if he were misbehaving."

"So it's Eli who is the problem, then," Samantha guessed. "What is that man doing? Is he giving you a hard time?"

"Yes. No. Not exactly."

"You sound less than confident about that answer. It's harder than you imagined it would be, isn't it? Working with Eli?" Her friend's voice, which had only moments ago been teasing, now lowered to a serious tone. What was she getting at?

"It's complicated. I don't think Eli has really been around dogs much before. This is all new to him."

"That isn't what I meant, and you know it."

"It isn't easy. Eli has the agility and ego of a pro athlete, and he's easily frustrated if he doesn't get something right the first time, or if Bullet doesn't act exactly as he expects."

Samantha chuckled. "He does have that male ego going, doesn't he? But I didn't mean that, either."

"What, then?" Mary wasn't sure she really wanted to know. She slid into a deck chair and stretched her legs out in front of her.

"I was actually thinking about high school. You had a real thing for Eli back then. A pretty solid crush, as I remember."

Mary stiffened. She was glad her friend wasn't here to see the expression that must have crossed her face. "What does that have to do with anything?"

"I'm only pointing out that as cute as Eli was in high school, he is all that and so much more as a man. You have to admit he's one fine-looking fellow," Samantha teased. "With the way you were hung up on him in high school, I thought you might have a little trouble having a working relationship with the guy. He has got to be distracting, right? I mean, that thick dark hair alone is enough to send a woman's heart into spasms—and don't get me started on those baby blues."

"I don't—" Mary coughed and hesitated while she struggled to form the words "—have a thing for Eli."

That was the truth, wasn't it?

"Did you just blink?"

"What?" Mary sat bolt upright in her chair.

"You know that thing that you do when you get all melty over a guy. Blink. Blink. Blink."

Mary opened her eyes as wide as possible, until there was no possibility of her blinking. "I don't do that."

Samantha laughed. "Yes, you do. You're doing it right now."

"Am not. And you couldn't tell anyway. You can't even see me."

"No, but I'm sure you're trying not to blink at all right now."

Mary blinked. Twice. On purpose.

"I'm not going to push you on this, if you don't want to talk about it," Samantha assured her.

Mary snorted. "Well, then, that's a relief."

"But if you need someone to talk to, you know you can count on me. I'm an expert in matters of the heart."

"I suppose because you're married?"

"No. Because I traveled a long, hard road to get here. It took me too much time to trust what I have with Will. I made everything that happened into far more of an issue than things needed to be."

"Not every woman is lucky enough to have their future husband—ex-army, I might add—

just walk in off the street and introduce himself, the way yours did."

"Don't I know it. And I thank God every day for Will. The hard part was for me to admit I had feelings for him." Her voice suggested she wasn't talking only of herself.

"And you think I'm doing the same thing with Eli?"

"I didn't say that." Samantha paused, and then chuckled. "Yes. Yes, I did. But I won't push you. Not now, in any case. Anyway, that's not why I called. I have a favor to ask you."

"Name it."

"I promised Alexis that I'd be there to help her take in her next batch of kids at Redemption Ranch, but Will had already made plans for us to be out of town that day. Do you think you might be able to step in for me and help Alexis out?"

"Sure thing." Mary relaxed into the chair and cradled the phone close to her ear, relieved that the spotlight was no longer on her and her pathetic excuse for a social life. Besides, she loved helping out their friend with the teenage reform program she ran through her ranch. "When do you need me?"

"Three weeks from Saturday. She's got seven new kids coming in. If you ask me, I think she's going to need all the help she can get. I can't imagine working with that many juvenile delinquents at the same time. I'd pull my hair out."

"Alexis doesn't see them that way."

"Bless her heart. She really does wear blinders—with amazing results. God has used her in magnificent ways with those teens. And they're the first to admit it—after she's finished with them, anyway." Samantha chuckled, and Mary laughed with her.

"I'd be happy to lend a hand. Tell her I'll be there." Mary paused as Bullet came dashing around the corner of the house, soap suds still clinging to his head and neck, and water dripping from his fur.

"Now, what in the world?" she mumbled, patting her knee and making kissing noises to beckon the dog to her side.

"What happened?" Samantha asked.

"It's nothing. Listen, I have something I need to take care of right now. I'll see you in church on Sunday?"

"If not before. Love ya, Mary."

"You, too, hon." Mary rang off and stuffed her phone into the back pocket of her blue jeans.

"Hey, buddy," she said to Bullet, rubbing her palm down the dog's side, wiping off some of the residual suds. "You've got secrets to tell, don't you, you impish dog. What did you do to Eli?"

* * *

"Sorry for the interruption," Mary apologized as she entered the laundry room with Bullet at her heel. "I didn't mean to leave you on your own here."

"Everything okay?"

Mary tittered and waved her hand in a dismissive motion. "Samantha was having one of her dramatic moments, and she needed to talk. You know how she can be sometimes. By the way, Bullet came out to find me after you finished with his bath. I don't want to sound critical, but you missed a few spots."

Eli sputtered.

She glanced up, and her mouth gaped as her gaze covered the chaotic scene.

"What happened in here?" He could see that she was desperately trying to restrain a chuckle, but amusement underlined every word, not to mention the way her eyes were glittering. "Did the sprayer explode on you?"

Eli combed his fingers through his wet hair, wishing the ground would open up and swallow him whole. No way he'd get out of this one with his pride unscathed.

"I forgot to check the temperature before I sprayed the dog," he said with a chagrined shrug. "The water was freezing. Bullet objected."

Laughter escaped Mary's lips, and Eli

scowled, though he couldn't really be angry. He had to admit—*privately*—that it was funny, but she was enjoying the moment far too much for his liking. His skin was prickling and not only from the cold.

"You'll get better at it," she promised, moving to the table and pulling a towel from one of the folded piles. She didn't seem to notice that the rest of the load consequently fell over into a disorderly heap. Eli resisted the urge to straighten it himself.

She wrapped the towel around Bullet and rubbed his fur dry. The dog was clearly enjoying her ministrations.

It just figured. Eli couldn't even do a bath right. Not like Mary. He was jealous at how effortless it all was for her.

"You're welcome to grab a towel for yourself," she said, nodding toward the table. "Then if you want, I can walk you through Bullet's dinner routine."

Eli lifted his chin, ignoring the frosty drops of water that trickled from the corner of his jaw. "I think I've had enough torture for one day, don't you?"

She leaned back to meet his gaze, crouching on her heels. "I suppose you have. I imagine you want to get home and out of those soppy clothes. As the old song goes, there's always tomorrow."

Tomorrow.

Mary made tomorrow sound like a good thing. For her, it was. He only hoped some of her enthusiasm would rub off on him.

Chapter Four

"Spread those boxes on either side of the dirt road there. We'll eventually be hiding Bullet's tennis ball in the one marked with a red *X*," Mary instructed Eli. "I've hollowed out some holes farther on, so we can do some underground work with him, too."

And you, she added silently. She held Bullet's lead and distracted him while Eli placed the boxes.

It was a beautiful Friday in early February, now three full weeks into their training period. Mary still occasionally noticed Eli's continued reticence in working with the dog, but she hadn't directly confronted him on it. She thought that might do more harm than good with a proud man like Eli. In any case, he and Bullet were finally making what she considered to be reasonable progress. She would have to be satisfied with that. They seemed to be working more and more as a unit with every day that passed. Now it was time to test the duo out in the open country, and teach them how to search and scan with real drugs.

"What's different about the one with the *X*?" he asked, jogging from one side of the road to the other and placing the containers where she'd indicated.

"It has been lined with trace amounts of a drug cocktail," she answered. "A mixture of marijuana, crack, cocaine and heroin."

His eyebrows rose in surprise, but he didn't question her—aloud, anyway. His shimmering deep blue gaze displayed both amusement and astonishment, and gave away exactly what he was really thinking.

She smothered a nervous chuckle. Eli had managed to put her on the spot without saying a word. No one else on the planet had the ability to rattle her so thoroughly. And working side by side with him for the past three weeks hadn't made it one bit easier for her.

"Obtained totally legally, compliments of the D.A.," she qualified with a nervous laugh. "They know about my training program and have licensed me to use small amounts of genuine drugs to train my dogs. Bullet has to learn to identify the scent of illegal substances."

Eli held up both hands, palms outward. "I would never have thought to suggest otherwise," he assured her with a cheeky grin.

She wrinkled her nose at him, just barely refraining from sticking out her tongue like a juvenile. Only her inherent dignity, bruised though it was, allowed her to maintain decorum.

As his comfort with the training had grown, Eli's tense anxiety of the first week had eased somewhat. This was good for making Bullet more comfortable with him. It was bad for Mary, though, since a more relaxed, more confident Eli was an Eli who flirted nonstop for the fun of it—and who seemed entirely too amused at the way it made her stammer. His swagger grew bigger every day.

Worse, he used flirting as a way to stall on working with Bullet. The connection between the man and dog still hadn't developed as fully as she'd hoped and figuring out what else she could try had her at her wit's end. Thus, today's lesson. Eli loved being a cop—if the proof of Bullet's potential usefulness out in the field didn't win him over, nothing would.

"Tell the truth. You did wonder where I'd gotten my hands on illegal drugs." She snorted in mock offense. "Like I bought them off the street or something. Really, Eli."

His lips twitched and his smile widened, if that were possible. "I've known you since you were knee-high to a grasshopper," he reminded her. "You could win the award for Most Integrity, if Serendipity had such a thing."

Mary creased her brow. That should have been a compliment, so why didn't it feel like one? Her skin itched. She was vitally aware how self-conscious she was around Eli, and she couldn't always tell when he was teasing her. Was it possible that he was mocking her for being such a Goody Two-shoes?

No. Not Eli. He wasn't that kind of man. He couldn't be intentionally cruel. It wasn't in his nature.

"Has anyone ever told you that you take things far too seriously?" He tilted his head, his gaze narrowing on her, speculative and gleaming, immediately followed by another bold— and *annoying*—grin.

Mary pushed her glasses up her nose with her index finger and shifted her gaze away from him so he wouldn't see the change in her expression. He hadn't a clue that he'd hit her where it hurt, smack-dab in the red zone of her insecurities. Of course she took his opinion of her too seriously. She'd been doing that for years.

Even when she was a child, she had hid her own perceived frailties behind the comfort of her more boisterous and outgoing friends. Both Samantha and Alexis were bubbly, vivacious, glass-half-full women whom everyone in town loved and respected. Mary couldn't help it if she'd been standing behind the door when God passed out confidence. The only thing she was fully confident in was her work—and that was what this afternoon was all about.

It wasn't as if this were a special occasion— it wasn't a date or anything. Not even remotely close. She was, for all intents and purposes, Eli's boss at the moment, and it was her job to make a K-9 unit out of him and Bullet. That was a serious business which needed her complete and comprehensive focus.

Not that Eli was in any position to accuse her of taking it too seriously. Eli was the poster child for an overachiever with perfectionist tendencies. He had to be the best at everything he did. Best football player. Best motorcycle rider. Best cop.

And now, best K-9 handler. Maybe that's why he sometimes appeared so brusque when he was around the dog. It was a good working theory.

"We're going to be learning how to scan and search today." Nothing like completely ignoring his statement and redirecting, but she didn't have a better solution.

"Scan as in having Bullet search for drugs?"

"Exactly."

"Cool. That sounds fun. Now we're getting to the good stuff."

Mary chuckled and shook her head. His reaction was far better than she'd anticipated. She was glad he'd taken her lead on the conversation. This was the first time Eli had displayed genuine interest in the procedures she had been teaching him. "Haven't you learned by now? It's all good stuff."

"Yeah, but this is where the bad guys meet their match. We're gonna take 'em down, aren't we, Bullet?"

The dog barked and wagged his tail so hard his whole back end was a blur.

"See there?" Eli crowed. "Bullet agrees with me."

"Of course he does. You guys are partners, right? I told you a little enthusiasm would go a long way."

Understanding flooded Eli's gaze. Mary felt the turning point as genuinely as if they'd staked a flag and claimed the area. She hadn't been making nearly enough progress with Eli's mind-set, and then suddenly, there it was.

He got it.

"So the first thing I want to do is throw his tennis ball for him a few times. Remember to praise him when he brings it back to you."

And then it was gone.

His smile disappeared, and he sounded genuinely disappointed. "I thought you said we were finally going to start learning to search for the real thing."

"We'll get to it, I promise."

He shrugged, resigned but not happy to be having playtime as their warm-up rather than jumping right into the work as he'd hoped for. His attitude frustrated Mary. There was so much he still didn't get. Would he ever learn to trust her?

"Fetch? Uh, I mean, *apport?*"

"Nice Dutch," she commented, drawing out the words. "Apparently *someone* doesn't list patience as one of the primary virtues on his résumé."

"No. Nope. Can't say that I do. I stick with my true fortes. Remarkably charming. Devastatingly handsome."

"And yet so humble."

He wagged his eyebrows.

She shook her head and chuckled. "Stop giving me grief and toss the ball for Bullet. It's an important step in the process, warming him up before the *real deal*. We're getting him focused on his ball. Trust me."

Eli grumbled under his breath, but at least he threw the ball. Mary rolled her eyes. Exasperating man. Really. It was lucky for him he was cute, or she might just trash this whole idea.

"Are we warmed up yet?" he asked less than a minute later.

Less than a minute. Good grief. The man simply would not learn.

"I suppose we can move on," she agreed, even though she usually spent a good quarter of an hour playing fetch before moving her dogs on to another assignment.

"Awesome." He jogged up in front of her with Bullet at his heel, both of them bright-eyed and ready to go. She couldn't tell who was more eager to play the next game—or as Eli would prefer she say, to do the work.

"All right, then. I'll distract Bullet while you sneak his ball into the box marked with the red *X.* We don't want to let him know which box in which to look for his ball. He needs to use his nose."

"Is that safe for Bullet?"

"Perfectly," she assured him, glad that Eli cared enough to think of Bullet's safety. "The point of this exercise is that he learns to associate his tennis ball with certain scents. After a while, he'll search for those scents even without his ball in play."

"Gotcha. Makes sense. Can't wait to see it in action."

While Mary drew Bullet's attention away from what Eli was doing, he trotted down the road and dropped the tennis ball into the marked box. When he returned, she handed him Bullet's lead and nodded toward the first box on the road.

"You're going to lead him beside the box you want him to scan. In essence, you're showing him where you want him to work, and then you'll step aside and let him do his job. In addition to using the verbal command *reveiren,* which is Dutch for *search,* I find it helpful to use a hand signal to indicate the general area you want him to cover. I use a simple sweeping hand motion."

She demonstrated, and Eli copied the gesture.

"The trick is not to use your own body language to give the hit away. Obviously, in this practice session, you know where you hid the ball, but Bullet doesn't. You want him to figure it out with his nose, not by you giving him silent indications. During a legitimate search, you won't have any idea where the drugs are hidden, or even if they are present at all. You'll need to be able to trust Bullet's instincts and of course his encompassing sense of smell."

"What will happen when he finds the ball?"

Mary smiled to herself. Eli had said *when* he finds the ball, not *if.* He was starting to trust

Bullet without even realizing he was doing so. *Progress*.

"He'll indicate a hit with a firm sit. That said, you'll want to be ready with a correction, if necessary. If for some reason he doesn't sit, or if he shifts his hind end around or doesn't stay until you've released him, you'll want to be right on top of it. He's a great dog, but he's still in his puppy stage. Sometimes he gets a little overexcited."

Eli approached the first box and gestured with his arm. "Bullet, *reveiren*."

"Excellent! Strong, solid command. He's watching you. Stay out in front of him. Keep leading. Praise, praise, praise."

"Good boy, good boy," Eli responded, high-pitched and full of excitement. He was just getting warmed up. He was clearly in his element doing actual police work. There was a bounce in his step and a gleam in his eye that had been missing from his earlier sessions. He led Bullet to the next box and repeated the scan motion. By the time they'd reached the subsequent box, the energy coming off the pair was almost palpable.

For the first time since they'd started, Eli and Bullet were working as a legitimate team, both focused on the same goal instead of one always getting in the way of the other.

Mary's heart soared with encouragement. She'd begun to doubt her own abilities, to despair of ever being able to train a man-dog unit. Maybe they would work out after all and her goals were more than a hopeless pipe dream. She hoped so, for all of their sakes.

Her breath caught in her throat as Eli and Bullet neared the drug box. She watched carefully to discern whether Eli might be giving Bullet subtle clues in his body language, but he acted exactly the same as he'd done with the others.

Bullet took one sniff and immediately went into overdrive. His whole body was quivering, but he gave a solid sit.

"Look at that!" Eli exclaimed. "Good boy, good boy, good boy!"

"Quickly now. Grab the ball out of the box and bounce it for him as a reward. Keep going with your praise. You're both doing great."

For once, Eli didn't appear to mind following her instructions. The high-toned baby voice he was using was absolutely adorable—or rather, the man doing the speaking was adorable, though she was fairly certain he wouldn't want to know that. Could she help it if her heart skipped a beat or two?

"That was *awesome*," he called out enthusiastically as Bullet returned the ball to him. He didn't hesitate to take the ball out of the dog's mouth. In fact, he didn't even appear to notice he was doing so. That was an enormous improvement from his first day, and a big check mark on Mary's review clipboard.

"It kind of was, wasn't it?" Her pulse was racing. She was catching the unit's excitement.

"Can we do it again?"

Enthusiasm. Check.

"Absolutely. I've already dug a few holes just up the road here. I buried boxes there early this morning. All we have to do is move the drug box up to the hole I've hollowed out for it and spread a little dirt around it for cover."

Eli picked up the marked box and they started up the road in companionable silence. It was especially gratifying to see Bullet padding along at Eli's heel instead of hers. Apparently the dog was learning how to trust the man. She was glad their mutual dependence on each other was growing.

When they arrived at the open hole, Eli dropped the box, hid the tennis ball inside and brushed dirt over the top. Then they returned to where Mary had marked the beginning of the course, and Eli and Bullet began a new scan.

Mary gave herself a mental pat on the back. Eli and Bullet made it look easy, but Mary knew from experience how much skill it took to properly search with a K-9. For a man who appeared less than enthusiastic about his new position on the K-9 unit, he certainly had a knack for it. There was something inherently natural and organic about the way the two moved in synchronicity. Bullet was completely focused on Eli's command, and Eli didn't waver.

When they neared the marked box, Bullet immediately marked the hit, sitting prettily. When the dog's rump momentarily left the ground in his excitement, Eli gently corrected him, and then bounced the ball for him, lining the air with his high-pitched praise.

When Mary approached, Eli picked her up by the waist and turned her around with an exuberant whoop. "We've got it!"

"You've got it," she agreed with light laughter, her heart revving like a race car. He was still holding her well above the ground, with her feet dangling in the air. The woodsy scent of his aftershave colored her senses, making her breathless and light-headed. "You've still got me, too."

He beamed down at her and then his eyes widened. For the first moment after their gazes locked, there was just the two of them, breathing as one. The air was thick and alive between them. Every one of her senses expanded and flittered wildly, rooted only in Eli. There was something…*more*…between them. Mary felt that unexplained something. It was there in Eli's warm gaze. Slowly, carefully, he lowered her to the ground, his arms lingering around her waist even after she was back on her feet.

"I…er…sorry," he stammered. "I guess I got a little too caught up in the moment. I apologize."

"Nothing to apologize for," she assured him, straightening her silk scarf over her royal-blue cardigan and wondering if he noticed the blush on her cheeks. And did he know he'd put it there? She laughed nervously and fought the urge to cover her face with her palms.

She had never felt so discombobulated in all of her life. Happy, sad, confused, excited, despondent and yet with a singular, joyfully vivid portrait of what had happened between them. She couldn't stay here, in this emotional place—not without risking much more than just her business.

"I'm glad to see some enthusiasm out of you for a change." Distance. She needed to put distance between them, if only in her words.

"I'm just happy to be doing real work. *For a change,*" he quipped back, quirking that adorable grin of his. Apparently he hadn't been as affected by what had happened as she had been, which led her to question if she might have imagined the whole *moment* altogether. Was it all in her head?

Of course it was. *You're not his type. You never have been.*

She was ashamed of herself for making something out of nothing. Now she wanted to move on—and away from her own idiocy.

She started to correct him, but then closed her mouth without saying a word. She could talk until she was blue in the face and never convince him that tossing a tennis ball was *work.* At least he was beginning to associate it with rewarding Bullet for a job well done. If that wasn't work, she didn't know what was, but there was no sense in arguing with him about it. Besides, there'd been amusement in his tone. Maybe he was just teasing her. He still had that undecipherable gleam in those blue eyes—the one she inevitably misinterpreted.

Reality? Check, please.

"What's next?" he asked eagerly, bouncing on his toes in roughly the same rhythm as Bullet's wagging tail.

"As you've witnessed, I've trained Bullet to associate his tennis ball with the scent of illegal drugs. Now we'll get Bullet to mark a hit on the drugs without the use of his ball—except as his reward, of course.

"There are a couple of junked autos farther up this road. I've planted the scent in one of them, but I'm not going to tell you which one.

You and Bullet will have to search the vehicles to find the plant. It's probably one of the more frequent actions you will have to perform on the police force, since you will be the only K-9 unit available for miles around."

"At least until you get contracts with the other departments," he reminded her, wagging his eyebrows. His face was virtually radiating with another stellar grin.

"Thank you for the vote of confidence." She didn't know if she could stand it if he smiled at her again. Her heart just kept leaping, as if on his command, no matter how she reprimanded it. Where Eli was concerned, she simply had no control over her emotions. Which meant working with him was the most dangerous— and painful—thing she'd ever done.

"Believe it," Eli assured her, tossing the ball ahead of him down the road for Bullet to fetch.

"Thank you," she repeated, feeling foolish for not having something clever to say. "Are you ready for this next go-round with Bullet?"

His lips twitched. "I don't know. It depends. I've never been very good at tests. Is that what this is?"

Eli's skin prickled as he noted the extended pause before Mary answered him. And she wouldn't meet his eyes—never a good sign.

"I'm not testing you, exactly," she promised him. "I'm trying to mimic what you're likely to face in the field. A lot rides on how well you and Bullet are able to execute your orders together as a unit. You aren't going to know whether or not drugs are present when you're searching a parking lot full of cars or the lockers at the high school."

"You have a point," Eli admitted. He felt like his performance had improved with the day's work, but he didn't want to ruin it by blowing this next search. If he was going to be graded, that upped the ante. He wasn't happy with any less than the best score possible, which meant he had to ace this exercise.

He was fairly positive he hadn't given Bullet any body language clues during the past two searches, but he *had* known where the drugs were hidden, so anything was possible. Now he had to rely entirely on the interplay between himself and Bullet, and he wasn't entirely confident they would succeed.

It all came down to one thing—he was being forced to trust the dog.

Now, there was irony. He never would have imagined himself in this situation, and yet here he was. Not only working with a dog but depending on him.

"It's about a half mile. Do you want to hop in

my vehicle and drive down the road, or would you rather walk?" Mary asked.

Eli removed the ball from Bullet's jaws and heaved it as hard as he could into the brush. Bullet bounded after it, his tail wagging. He was no longer white-knuckled every time his hand got near the dog's chops, which was really saying something. "We can walk. It's a nice day out."

"I think so, too. Sometimes I bring Sebastian out here to walk and spend some quiet time with God."

As they started down the road, Eli glanced in her direction, but she wasn't looking at him. In fact, she seemed to be looking anywhere *but* at him, lost in whatever it was that she was ruminating over. His gaze swept over the curl of her light brown hair and lingered on the dimple in her chin that perfectly divided her heart-shaped face. She was a pretty woman—not with the striking look-at-me way her sister, Natalie, had about her—but with a gentle, unassuming beauty that snuck up on a man and grabbed him from behind, and then wouldn't let go.

"What are you thinking about?" he asked, his voice taking on a low, husky timbre.

She glanced up at him, surprise widening her emerald gaze.

"Oh… I… Well," she stammered before looking away again. "I don't think I ought to say."

"I'm sorry. I didn't mean to intrude upon your privacy." Eli chastised himself, but in the same instant, he also felt the slap of rejection. Irrational, but there it was.

"It's not that." Her cheeks took on a lovely rose hue. "I just don't— I was thinking about Natalie," she blurted.

"Oh." Eli's heart slammed to a halt in his chest.

"See? Now I'm the one who is sorry. I'm sure her name is the last you'd like to hear right now. Or ever."

That much was true enough, but it wasn't Mary's fault she was related to a self-absorbed shrew like Natalie.

"It's okay for you to talk about her to me," he said. "She's not my favorite subject, sure, but I can't pretend nothing ever happened between me and Natalie, or that she is not your sister." He swallowed the well of humiliation bubbling in his throat. "Family is family, and blood is blood. You can't walk away from those kinds of bonds. I get that."

"It was just so *unfair* of her to do that to you."

Eli let out a surprised chuckle. For some reason, he hadn't expected Natalie's own sister to side with him. He'd assumed she would think, as most of the town did, that he was somehow at fault for the sudden breakup.

"You think so?" he asked, amazed by where this conversation was leading.

"I *know* so," she replied adamantly. "Natalie may be beautiful on the outside, but she has a real selfish streak. Even when she was a little girl, she never thought of anyone but herself. I can't say I was completely surprised that she dropped you like a hot potato when a better offer came along."

Ouch. Her words stung, even if she was telling the truth.

She sucked in an audible breath and clapped her hands over her mouth, groaning from deep in her throat.

"Oh, I am so sorry. That did *not* come out the way I intended."

Eli dropped one shoulder and scoffed. "No biggie."

"Yes, it is. Eli—" She stopped walking and reached for his arm, pulling him to face her. "That *man* is not the better catch. Natalie saw nothing but the dollar signs in his eyes and the cash protruding from his pocket. She didn't care what kind of man she was getting—or giving up. I think she passed up the best thing that ever happened to her when she walked away from you, but I can't be angry with her for that—

she'll realize what she lost someday, and that'll be punishment enough. What still makes me mad is her lack of kindness in the matter. She was downright cruel to you, and there's no excuse for that."

Eli felt a genuine smile curl his lips. He cleared his throat, which suddenly felt grazed and thick with emotion. "Well, I'm glad you think so."

Her normally pale complexion turned a deep shade of burnished red, and the apples of her cheeks were the colors of—well, apples. Though she was obviously embarrassed that she'd spoken so passionately, he couldn't help but feel pleased, both at her clear opinion that he was the better man and at her anger on his behalf over the way he'd been treated. It was nice to know she cared.

She gave an uneasy nod and pointed across the grassland. "We go off-road from here for about another quarter of a mile."

Eli turned in the direction she indicated, focusing on where he placed his steps. The terrain was difficult. Black-tailed prairie dogs had spread out over the area, their colony marked at odd intervals by holes and mounds. He was wearing steel-toed work boots, which made navigation relatively easy, but Mary was wearing some kind of dainty slip-on shoe, which made her walk far more treacherous.

"Be careful," Eli warned, reaching for her hand. "The footing is a little tricky in some spots. These prairie-dog holes are everywhere."

Mary laughed. "Thank you, but I'm practically a mountain goat. I come out here all the time to— *Oh!*"

She sidestepped a prairie-dog hole, only to have her foot land squarely on a patch of loose gravel. Her ankle turned, and it was only thanks to the fact that Eli had his hand in hers that she didn't land on her backside.

"Are you okay?" Eli asked, lowering her gently to the ground.

She scoffed and shook her head. "Other than my dignity? Yeah, I'm okay."

Eli knelt to examine her ankle, which was already swelling and turning a concerning color of purple.

"I don't think so," Eli contended. "If I'm not mistaken, you've sprained it pretty bad. Hopefully it's not worse than that."

"It's nothing," she denied, rolling onto her knees. Shaky and using Eli's shoulder as a prop, she tried to stand. A distressed little mew escaped from her throat when she put weight on her ankle. She sank back down onto the dry grass with a discouraged sigh.

"We'd best get you to the doctor," Eli said, not asking for permission before scooping her into his arms. There was no way he was going to let her walk in this condition, though he knew she was stubborn enough to try. And he wasn't going to leave her alone to go retrieve her vehicle, either.

"Eli, you can't *carry* me," she protested against his chest.

"I don't see why not. We've got to get back to your SUV, and you aren't going to be walking." He started tramping back down the road.

"I can walk. I'll lean on you," she protested. "I'm far too heavy for you to carry all the way back."

"Are you kidding me right now?" Eli snickered through his teeth. "You're as light as a feather." He swung her around until she squealed, just to make his point.

He didn't know why she was creating such a fuss. If he was having a problem with anything, it wasn't her weight. The soft musk of her perfume was doing a number on him, but he wasn't going to complain about that.

Mary sighed in resignation. "At least don't make me go to the doctor. My ankle isn't broken, I promise. See, I can move it."

She rotated her ankle in a small circle. He

didn't miss the grimace of pain that crossed her face, but he didn't comment on it, either.

"There's ice in the cooler I put together for our lunch," she continued. "We can pack my ankle, and I'll rest while we eat."

"That sounds good for a start," Eli agreed. "I'm starving. But I'm declaring it to be the end of our workday today. You're not going back out on that ankle—you ought to keep it elevated for at least the rest of the day, probably longer. At the bare minimum we need to wrap your ankle in a bandage. So after lunch, I'm taking you home. No more resistance, okay?"

"But what about your bike? You can't leave it out here."

"Sure I can. No worries. I'll get my sister to drive me out here later to pick it up."

"But—"

"Will you please stop arguing with me? I'm a stubborn man. You aren't going to get anywhere with me, so you may as well save your breath and accept your fate." Her attitude was frustrating…but also oddly refreshing. He'd never had a woman argue so hard against letting him take care of her. The women he usually dated were only too willing to have him wait on them hand and foot. He had to admit, it was a pleasant change to spend time with someone who didn't insist on her own needs coming first.

As they reached Mary's vehicle, he gently placed her on the open tailgate while he spread a blanket in the bed of the SUV. Bullet curled up under the tailgate and promptly went to sleep, his tennis ball still in his mouth. Eli laid out the fare she had packed for them—bread, American cheese, hard salami, turkey, ham, veggies, chips and soda. His stomach rumbled.

She laughed. "I guess you really are hungry."

"Hey, I worked hard out there today. I deserve my appetite." He wrapped some ice in a dish towel and packed it around her ankle.

"Thank you," she whispered.

"That feel okay to you?"

"It's fine. Please stop fussing over me."

"So what if I want to fuss over you a little bit? You're hurt. I'm here. I'm gonna take care of you. End of story."

She looked away, but not before he spotted tears, her eyes awash in green.

"What's the matter? What can I do for you? Is it your ankle? I think I have some painkillers in the glove compartment."

She sniffed. "No. My ankle is fine. I just— well, thank you."

"You already said that."

"I did, didn't I? I'm starting to repeat myself, and that's never pretty. I'm sure you don't want to be stuck out here with a blubbering female."

Instead of replying, Eli stacked a sandwich for her. She was right about him not being comfortable with her tears, but that was because he didn't know what he could do to fix her problem.

He didn't even know what the problem *was*. If she wasn't crying because her ankle was hurting her, then why *was* she crying? What was wrong with her? She wasn't going to let him take her to the doctor, and frankly, he didn't know what else to do for her.

He handed her a sandwich, opened a bag of chips for her and popped the top on a soda can. Then he did the same for himself.

"I feel like a clumsy idiot," she admitted, brushing her shoulder-length curls back behind her ear. "I really do come out here all the time, and I've never had the least bit of a problem before. Talk about humiliating."

"We all stumble once in a while." He realized as he said the words that they were as true for him as they were for her. Literally and metaphorically.

"It's a good thing God is here to pick us up when we fall. And in this case, I was fortunate to have you around, as well."

He chuckled. "Anything I can do to help."

"If I'm not careful, I'm going to thank you

again. And I know you don't want to hear it. So let's talk about you and Bullet."

Eli's day had been going so well. Why was there always a twinge of discomfort every time he thought about Bullet? Even after all this time in the dog's company. He liked Bullet, most of the time, but that didn't take away the organic discomfort he sometimes felt. It disgusted him that he was still bothered by his stupid phobia.

"What about us? Is it time for our performance review? Should I be taking notes?"

"No, nothing like that." She laughed, but it was a nervous sound. "I have no notes. You two worked really well together today. You acted as a unit, which is why I think the time has come for you to make Bullet a permanent part of your life."

"What does that mean?" He and Bullet were already together every working hour. As relaxed as he'd been moments before, he was equally as uptight right now. His shoulders rippled with tension.

"It's time for you to make Bullet an official part of your family. He'll be living with you on a full-time basis from now on. That's how it goes with K-9 units. You get the benefit of having Bullet with you even when you're off duty."

No one had mentioned that part of the bargain when he'd taken this promotion. Why did he have to live with the dog? She might think he was ready, but he knew he was not.

"No."

The word was out of his mouth before he thought better of it.

"What?" Clearly Mary hadn't anticipated his objection.

"I don't mean no, no," he amended hastily. "I'm only saying that I'm not ready for him yet. I haven't prepared my place. It's not…dog-proofed. And I don't have anyplace for him to sleep or any food for him or anything."

"I've seen your apartment, Eli," Mary reminded him. She and her friends Samantha and Alexis—known collectively in town as the Little Chicks—had visited during the occasional party he'd hosted over the years, and now that he thought about it, Mary had once brought him homemade chicken soup when he'd missed Sunday services because of pneumonia.

"And?" He didn't mean to make the word sound like a challenge, but he knew it had come out that way.

"And you don't have to do anything special to dog-proof the place. I've never seen a more spit-polished home in my life. You've seen my house. If mine is dog-proofed, then yours passes with flying colors."

She had him there.

"Yeah, but the rest of it—"

"Is being supplied by the police force. I've got a nice little care package waiting for you back at my place. All the essentials. No worries."

No worries.

Except being on his own with a K-9 he didn't entirely trust. Bullet had never shown any sign of aggression toward him, but that didn't mean it wouldn't happen when they were alone together in his apartment, without Mary's confident dog-demeanor to keep Bullet at bay.

It was as if she'd splashed cold water in his face. He'd been thinking more about how his day had gone with Mary than how things were working out with Bullet. And now, suddenly, it was all about the dog.

He would never sleep again.

Chapter Five

As she drove the short distance to Alexis's Redemption Ranch, Mary lifted her soft peach-colored silk scarf to her nose and inhaled the woodsy smell of Eli's aftershave. It had been eight days since she'd worn it—since the day she'd twisted her ankle—but Eli's unique scent still permeated the fabric.

He was a hero, that one. She'd known it since she was a fifteen-year-old wallflower at the town's Sweetheart Social. His actions of eight days ago only confirmed that verdict in her mind.

At the three-way stop, she closed her eyes for a moment, remembering the tender way he'd carried her back to her vehicle, the way he'd fussed over her and treated her as if she were delicate and valuable. As if he cared for her— really cared. She'd never felt as cherished by anyone as she had in that moment.

And therein lay the problem. She had no doubt her romantic ramblings were not at all the impressions Eli had intended to leave with her.

He's a good guy, she reminded herself. That was the beginning and the end of the matter, with the strongest punctuation her mind could muster. She was fluffing the middle with her fertile imagination. And she had to get over it. Now.

Especially since she'd completely trampled over whatever *moment* they may or probably had not had. She had panicked, opened her big mouth and said the first thing she could think of to stop his fussing in its tracks.

I think the time has come for you to make Bullet a permanent part of your life.

Could she have uttered any more foolish words? Short of *You were the first guy I ever loved,* she couldn't think of a single thing that would make Eli run away faster and farther.

She'd known he was uneasy with the dog. She'd watched him, gauged his resistance. Knew that it still lingered just under the surface, even if she still did not know why.

But once the words had come out, there was no way to take them back. For a moment, she'd almost hoped that he'd surprise her by taking the news well. She thought she'd seen major progress, given the way Eli and Bullet were working as a unit that day. She'd thought Eli was growing more comfortable with Bullet, as the dog certainly was with him.

She'd been sorely mistaken on that point.

Eli had taken the dog into his home, and though he hadn't complained, it was clear he wasn't pleased with the arrangement. It had been pure torture working with him all week.

Adding on to the renewed tension on Eli's part, Mary had had to deal with her own tangled feelings. Her mind kept returning to the memory of Eli catching her in his arms, carrying her with such gentleness, taking care of her like she mattered to him. Over and over again, she told herself not to make so much of it—to remember that Eli had no romantic interest in her at all, and it would be ridiculous to fall back into her silly crush on him again. She wasn't a child anymore. She could be sensible, and remain in control of herself and her feelings... couldn't she?

Apparently not, since she'd spent the whole week worrying that she would accidentally display her unresolved feelings for Eli in a glance or an action.

She had been looking forward to an Eli-free weekend. The stress of being with him was almost too much for her, and she desperately needed the downtime to rest and recuperate, so she could find a better angle with which to approach this sticky situation.

Mary's sigh echoed through the cab as she turned her SUV onto the long unpaved driveway that led to Redemption Ranch, which Alexis and her twin sister, Vivian, had inherited from their grandfather. Unfortunately Vivian had no interest in the land, much less the ministry for troubled youth that was part and parcel of Alexis's life and heart. Like Natalie, hair, fashion and high living were the bedrocks of Vivian's existence. Perhaps Mary and Alexis's shared experiences with their sisters was one of the reasons they'd bonded so closely as friends.

Mary pulled to the side of the house and braked suddenly, finding a large truck already parked in her usual space. Was that Eli's?

She slid out of her vehicle and limped around to inspect the foreign truck. Slick, black and well waxed, the vehicle was rarely used because Eli preferred to ride his motorbike whenever the weather cooperated. Still, she'd seen it often enough to recognize it beyond a doubt.

Yes, that was Eli's vehicle, all right. The real question was why was he *here?* What was the strangest part of this was that Eli had known she was going to help Alexis with the intake of her teenagers this weekend, yet he'd never given her a single clue that he was going to be part of the experience himself.

What was going on?

For a brief moment she considered turning around and going back home without announcing her presence, but she quickly nixed that idea. She'd promised Samantha and Alexis, and she wasn't the type of woman to go back on her promises, even under duress—and Eli definitely qualified as duress.

Slightly more motivating was the moment she realized Eli was looking out Alexis's front window, his arm crooked to hold back the curtain. Bullet was with him, nosing the window with his feet propped on the sill. The dog's presence explained why Eli had brought his truck instead of his motorcycle.

And Eli was waving. At her.

He had the advantage over her. He'd known she would be here today. It almost seemed as if he'd been waiting for her.

She shook her head and scoffed at herself for not moving forward. Even if he wasn't staring right at her, which he was, what would be the point of avoiding him? She had to work with him practically every day as it was. Instead of reacting to her own fears and doubts, she ought to be thanking God for Eli's willingness to go above and beyond for Alexis and the teens.

Mary was being selfish, and she was better than that.

Eli opened the front door for her before she even knocked, with Bullet close at his heels.

"The kids haven't arrived yet. Alexis is back in the kitchen putting some finishing touches on some finger food for them," he said by way of greeting.

"Oh, yum. Pigs in a blanket, I hope. No one makes them like Alexis. I'm always first in line with my plate when she serves those up at community events."

Her face burned. She'd been speaking figuratively, of course, but she'd made herself sound like a cow desperate to stuff her face. She was already overly self-conscious about her weight without having to go and make herself out to be a glutton.

Surely Eli had been perfectly aware of the extra weight on her frame when he'd swept her off her feet after she'd sprained her ankle. As a woman who'd spent all her life struggling with her weight, *self-conscious* didn't even begin to cover it.

"You think she'd let us steal a couple before the teenagers get to them? You know how teenage boys are. One look and they'll be gone for sure." He put a hand at the small of her back and guided her toward the kitchen, leaning in close to her ear. "Should we be polite and ask, or..." He paused and winked at her. "I have a few stealthy moves I've perfected over the years, especially where food is concerned."

"And you, a cop. I should have you arrested." Mary laughed, amazed at the way Eli had managed to put her at ease. Had he recognized her discomfort and started cracking jokes to take the heat off of her? Or had he just missed her self-conscious drama moment altogether? Hopefully the latter.

"I think it's safe to say Alexis will share with us," she guessed.

Alexis appeared in the doorway that separated the dining room from the kitchen, bearing a large platter of pigs in a blanket and fresh-from-the-oven snickerdoodle cookies. She grinned, showing a line of naturally straight teeth, and extended the tray to them. She had one of those smiles that sent men reeling, but she was too preoccupied with her work here at the ranch to use that smile much.

"Alexis," she informed them, "can hear you two plotting out here." Her lips twitched with merriment. "Count yourselves blessed that I thought of you guys and planned ahead. One of each, cookies and piggies. Take your pick."

Mary hung back as Eli hovered over the platter, stretching out the time as he selected the biggest cookie available. He groaned in anticipation, then picked up the nearest pastry-covered sausage and popped the whole thing into his mouth at once, chasing it down with the cookie. One bite. Two. And it was gone.

Alexis swatted at him with her free hand. "Elijah Bishop!" she exhorted, playfully shaking her head. "Where are your manners? Didn't your mama teach you to chew your food before you swallow it?"

"My mama," Eli responded, one side of his lips creeping up as he took the tray from Alexis and offered it to Mary, "taught me how to *appreciate* good food. And to thank the chef when I'm finished." Alexis was tall, so he didn't have far to lean to buss her noisily on the cheek. "This is well worth a thank-you."

Alexis giggled. Coming from anyone else, a thirtyish-year-old woman giggling would have sounded ridiculous or coy, but Alexis's laughter was at once joyful and flirtatious, and without a note of pretension. It was no wonder Eli was grinning at her like she was today's top headline.

Despite the fact that his attention had drifted to Alexis, Eli still held the platter out to Mary. She resisted the urge to decline a treat. She was the one who had been raving about the pigs in a blanket to begin with, and she wasn't kidding when she said they were out-of-this-world delicious. It would be silly not to take one. She selected the smallest one and delicately nibbled on an end.

The silent exchange between Eli and Alexis shouldn't have surprised her. Now *there* was a woman who fit Eli's profile. Alexis with her tall, lithe body and beautiful blond hair—ponytailed at the moment, but long and cascading when she let it down—was definitely his kind of woman. Mary could see Eli falling for her, if he ever got over Natalie, that is. He and Alexis would make a cute couple. But Mary couldn't repress a shiver at the prospect.

Mary took another bite of her sausage and nearly choked, barely able to swallow through her dry mouth. She adjusted her glasses. She was getting way ahead of herself, and it wasn't helping matters any. She was already hearing wedding bells for Eli and Alexis, which was a ridiculous waste of emotional energy. And that was *not* jealousy stabbing the inside of her rib cage.

Alexis reached for the tray. "Are you sure you don't want a snickerdoodle, honey?" she tempted, waving the cookies under Mary's nose.

Mary shook her head. "I'm good."

"Can I have her cookie, then?" Eli snatched

another snickerdoodle from the platter and popped it into his mouth.

"Smooth," Alexis admonished, chuckling and shaking her head. "Let me take this tray back to the kitchen." She made a face at Eli. "I wouldn't want to tempt you again. Besides, we ought to be out front when they come in. The kids should be here any moment now." Her blue eyes shimmered with excitement and anticipation. Working with troubled youth was truly her calling, evident in everything from her posture to the expression on her face. And Mary knew her heart—it was golden.

Just as they reached the front porch, a white van pulled slowly up the long driveway. It came to a stop in front of the house and seven teenagers piled out of the back end—four boys and three girls, and not a one of them looked happy to be there. The van driver, with a long-suffering sigh and an equally dire frown, began unloading the kids' suitcases, placing them on the edge of the concrete that surrounded Alexis's house.

Mary glanced at Alexis, but her elated expression hadn't changed. She was happy to meet these kids, even if they weren't so enthused to see her. In her place, Mary would have been terrified that she would be eaten alive. These teenagers had teeth.

It took a strong, confident woman to face the kinds of odds before Alexis. These young people didn't even look like they *wanted* to be helped. Mary knew she couldn't handle the kind of rejection Alexis must face on a daily basis, much less the bitter, entitled attitudes of youth born with the proverbial silver spoon in their mouths. They were here at Redemption Ranch to work off their misdemeanors from their juvenile records with community service. Roughing it wasn't generally their style—which was why Alexis's therapy was so successful. Hard work and tough love had the biggest impact on this kind of kid.

The boys were shouting and jostling each other. The girls had their noses glued to their fancy smartphones.

Alexis tried to get their attention with a wave of her hand, but she might as well not have bothered.

"If I could have your attention, please," she announced, but none of the teens were listening to her. Mary wondered what she could do to help round these kids up.

Eli put his fingers to his lips and blew a sharp, shrieking whistle that caught the attention of everyone from the van driver to the teenagers to Bullet, who sat down in front of Eli and cocked his head.

"Listen up," he ordered.

It wasn't a suggestion, it was a command, and apparently one that the kids took seriously. The boys stopped wrestling and turned their attention toward Eli. The girls looked up from their smartphones with barely masked curiosity.

"This is Miss Alexis Granger, and she will be your counselor and guide for the next four weeks. Show her respect. Listen to her. Do as she asks, or you'll ultimately answer to me."

Which wasn't entirely true—at the ranch, the buck stopped with Alexis—but Eli's threat seemed to work. The teenagers mumbled under their breaths and gave sullen nods. It was a hard lot. Mary wondered how Alexis would ever break through to them, especially without Eli always around to strong-arm them into complying.

"Welcome to Redemption Ranch," Alexis said. Her expression was still cheerful, but her voice carried more of an edge to it. "We'll be doing a lot of fun things together in this coming month. We've got all kinds of livestock for you to look after, and every one of you is going to learn how to ride and care for the horse to which you'll be assigned. This is a working ranch, so prepare yourselves for some hard work."

A collective groan came from the teens.

"You can always go back home to mommy

and daddy, and pick up trash along the highway for your community service," Alexis suggested wryly.

That got their attention.

"One other thing," she continued, gesturing toward one of the girls, who once again had her eyes glued to the phone in her hand.

Alexis bent her elbows and clasped one fist under her chin in a thoughtful pose. "There will be no cell phones during working hours. Calls and texts are allowed during your free time, but if I spot a cell phone when you're on my time, I will confiscate it, and you won't see it again until your month is up. Are we clear?"

The girl with the phone in her hand sniffed audibly. "Seriously?"

Alexis met the girl's gaze and arched one of her brows. The teen grumbled and reluctantly slid her phone into her back pocket.

"Don't worry about it. You'll be far too busy learning new things to have time to update your friends online."

"I don't like this," one of the boys grumbled. Like all of the teenagers present, he was wearing expensive preppy clothes—designer jeans and a pricey leather jacket. He had carefully spiked his gelled black hair and was sporting peach fuzz on his upper lip and around his sideburns. He'd clearly meant his comment for his friends, but Alexis picked up on it.

"You," she said, pointing right at the boy. "Have you ever been on a horse before today?"

The boy scoffed and toed the dirt like a bull getting ready to charge. "Not a chance, lady."

"That would be, 'No, ma'am,' to you," Eli corrected in a rich, no-nonsense rumble.

"No, ma'am," the boy responded in a broody mumble, not meeting any of the adults' eyes.

"Consider yourself blessed," Mary informed the boy. If she intended to be of any use to Alexis and the teens, she needed to jump into this conversation. "Alexis rounded up the best staff in Texas to teach y'all how to ride. Genuine cowboys."

To Mary's surprise, the loudmouthed boy raised his gaze, his eyes alight with reluctant interest.

"Real cowboys? Like roping cows and everything?"

"Just exactly like that," Mary assured him. "And if you cooperate with Alexis and work really hard, you might even get to try your hand at roping, too."

The boy nodded, though his posture remained reserved and his shoulders slouched.

"You'll get your mounts assigned to you tomorrow," Alexis promised them. "Before you can ride, you'll learn how to care for your horse."

All three of the teenage girls wrinkled their noses in unison. Mary chuckled under her breath. They had little idea what they were in for. Born and raised in Serendipity, she was intimately familiar with the unpleasant parts of caring for horses. Livestock were the warp and woof of the small ranching town.

"However," Alexis continued, holding up her hands to contain the groans of complaint. "I've brought along someone really cool for you to meet today. This," she said, gesturing toward Eli, "is Deputy Eli Bishop of the Serendipity Police Department and his K-9 partner, Bullet."

"You're a cop?" a young man with messy blond hair covered by a backward-facing baseball cap asked dubiously, sweeping his hat off and flicking his head to swish his hair out of his eyes.

"Better than that. A K-9 unit," Mary corrected proudly.

"In training." Eli grinned and winked at her.

The boys drew nearer to Eli, clearly interested in his career and his work with the dog, but the girls still hung back. Mary noticed that their gazes tended to rest more on Eli than on Bullet, though she couldn't really blame them for that. How many times had her own gaze drifted to Eli when she was supposed to be watching the interactions between him and his K-9? It wasn't every day a girl got to meet a real live hunky cop who looked like he just stepped off of the pages of a magazine.

Eli stepped into the proverbial limelight with gusto. "So this is my partner, Bullet. He's a Dutch shepherd. I even use Dutch commands with him. Bullet, *volg*."

To Mary's delight, the dog obeyed immediately, circling around Eli and then sitting at his left heel, his attention focused on Eli, waiting for his next command. Eli beamed.

He pulled an orange tennis ball out of the pocket of his black leather jacket. He displayed it at arm's length, shoulder high. Bullet's attention was immediately caught by the ball, but so were the teenagers'. The guys snickered. The girls giggled.

"This is Toby," Eli said, as if introducing them to a person.

Mary sputtered. "You named Bullet's tennis ball?"

"Better," Eli informed her with a comic grin. He turned to face her so she could take a gander at what the teenagers had already seen.

He'd drawn a funny face on the ball in permanent blue felt-tip pen, complete with eyebrows and a toothy jack-o'-lantern grin.

"Mary, this is Toby. Toby, meet Mary." He bounced the ball against the pavement and caught it again without changing the angle of the face on the ball. Mary wondered how long it had taken him to master that particular trick.

"Glad to meet you, Toby." Mary gave Toby an imaginary handshake and rolled her eyes at Alexis. "Eli—you felt inclined to name the tennis ball…. Why?"

Eli shrugged and bobbed his dark eyebrows. "I figured the four of us were going to be spending a lot of time together. It seemed only fitting that we named him."

"Bullet helped you choose a name, did he?"

"Well, sure. Bullet likes the name Toby, don't you, boy?"

Bullet assented with a wag of his tail. His front feet were fidgeting in excitement as he anticipated Eli throwing the ball for him.

"Wait. What do you mean, the four of you?"

"You, me, Bullet and Toby, of course."

"Right. Why didn't I know that?"

Mary took a seat on the porch, and for the next half hour, Eli and Bullet entertained the kids with various obedience exercises and games, getting the teens personally involved and teaching them a few things about how the K-9 program was connected to the police force.

After a few minutes, the girls had warmed up

to Bullet, petting him and fawning over him. The dog loved the attention and seemed to preen for the ladies, showing off his skills. Mary was surprised to see that the teen girls appeared unexpectedly shy and reserved around Eli, especially given the attitude they'd presented earlier. Mary suspected a lot of it was guff, and that underneath it all, the girls were intimidated by their new surroundings.

This must be how Alexis worked—chipping away at the teenagers' bad attitudes and resentments one loving minute at a time to find who they really were underneath. She was tough with the kids, but it was evident that she cared for them, and she suspected the teens saw it, too. There was already a shade of respect building between her and the kids. The pigs in a blanket and cookies she shared only helped her cause.

Eli was a natural when it came to working with the youth. He moved among them effortlessly, except for the occasional wrench when he had to take the ball from Bullet's mouth. There was still something off about their interaction.

"I think we should all get settled in before suppertime," Alexis finally announced. "You'll be eating your evening meal with me at the main house, and breakfast and lunch at the ranch hands' chow house located next to the bunkhouses. Just think of it. You'll get to experience how real cowboys eat. Cook is especially fond of beans and franks cooked over an open fire."

"Eww," exclaimed Allison, whom Mary had privately nicknamed Red due to her Irish coloring.

Alexis chuckled joyfully, and Mary and Eli joined in.

"You'll be meeting your overnight counselors at supper," Alexis informed the teens. "In the meantime, grab your bags. The bunkhouses are located out back."

The black-haired boy introduced as Matthew, but whom Mary privately thought of as Spike, crossed his arms and shook his head. "Maybe you don't know who we are. Get one of your old cowhands to take the bags for us. We're not gonna do it."

Uncomfortable with the disrespect Alexis was being shown, Mary adjusted her glasses and glanced first at Eli, and then at Alexis, wondering which one of them was going to handle the standoff.

Alexis merely arched a brow, the corner of her lip twitching as if something were amusing. "No? Well, then, your bags are going to stay exactly where they are right now. It's entirely up to you. I will say that I've heard there might be rain in the forecast for tonight. It gets a little muddy around here when the ground gets wet."

There was a tense moment where the teens stared openmouthed, first at Alexis, and then at each other, silently communicating between themselves.

Was she serious?

Mary could feel the tension in the air almost palpably, like static electricity, as the boy with the cap then turned and picked up his duffel bag. One by one, each of the teenagers took up their suitcases, until only Spike was left.

Mary almost felt sorry for the kid, now alone in his standoff. Something must have happened to the young man for him to be here in the first place, and since she couldn't walk in his shoes, she couldn't possibly know the truth of what lay behind his motivations. Compassion flooded her as she realized that this was how Alexis saw these teenagers—not as spoiled rich kids, but as God's special creations, each with a story of their own, in need of help and guidance to get on the right path.

Alexis ignored Spike and spoke to the rest of the group. "Fellas, if you'll follow Eli, he'll set you up in your bunkhouse. Ladies, Mary will show you to where you'll be settling in. I'm going to head back inside and get supper on the table for you all. I imagine you're hungry after that long trip."

The girls crowded around Mary, who offered to carry a couple of the smaller bags. To her surprise, the girls refused, as if they had something to prove to Alexis, or perhaps to themselves.

Maybe they did.

Red set her pace with Mary. "So that Eli guy," she said, trying too hard to sound casual and off the cuff and ending up sounding strained, unable to contain her curiosity. "He seems pretty cool, for a cop."

"He is." Mary grinned and nodded at the young woman's assessment. *And so much more,* she added silently.

"Is he married?" Red continued. No way to make *that* question sound casual.

Before Mary could answer, bleach-blonde Trish piped in from Mary's other side.

"Who cares, you idiot? He's *old.*"

Air hissed from between Mary's teeth as she attempted to contain her laughter. "Hey, now. Not *that* old."

Trish gazed at her speculatively, then smiled—a real smile that softened the edges of her face and transported her from pretty to beautiful.

"Sorry," Trish apologized. "No offense meant.

It's nothing personal. I'm just saying the cop is too old for Allison. I mean, come on. Really?"

"No offense taken," Mary assured her. "And I agree that Eli is much too old for Allison."

"My mom is twelve years younger than my dad," Allison informed Trish with a scoff.

"Yeah, and how is that working out for them? How many years have they been divorced now?" Trish shot back.

"Trish," Mary warned softly.

"Humph," Allison responded, dropping back to walk with Jemma, the third girl, who'd been lagging behind.

"What about you?" Trish queried, her voice more thoughtful than teasing.

Mary blanched and pretended not to know what Trish was asking. She didn't want to enter this territory at all. "What *about* me?"

"Do you like Eli? Are you two an item? He's not married, is he? I didn't see a ring." She rattled off the questions in rapid succession, not allowing Mary the time to answer even one of them.

When Trish finally paused, Mary didn't even know where to start. "Yes, I like Eli, although I suspect not in the way you mean." She wouldn't let herself, plain and simple. "No, he's not married. And what on earth made you ask if the two of us were an item?" Alexis was far closer to the type of woman Eli dated. Mary would think the teens would pair those two faster than they would think anything of her.

"I dunno," Trish admitted with a wry smile. "It was a feeling more than anything. Didn't you notice the way he was flirting with you and showing off for you with Toby, the tennis ball?"

Heat rushed to Mary's face, and she knew Trish would have no problem reading her reaction.

Eli? Flirting with her?

True, Eli liked to tease her by acting flirtatious, but it was clear he didn't mean anything by it. No. No way. If he'd been truly flirting with anyone today, it had been with Alexis—even going so far as to kiss her cheek. A friendly buss? Maybe. Or was it something else?

"You're mistaken," Mary rebutted, a bit harsher than she would have liked. She consciously softened and modulated her tone. "There's nothing between Eli and me. We work together, that's all." She pushed her glasses up her nose. She didn't want to talk about Eli anymore. She didn't even want to think about him. Shaking her head, she pointed to a long, rectangular cabin. Not terribly pretty, but functional, like an army barrack. "That's your new home for the next month. Come on in, and I'll show you around."

* * *

Eli showed the teenage boys—including the kid with the jacket, who did eventually back down and grab his own bag—to their bunks and instructed them when and where to go for supper. Leaving them to unpack and process their new surroundings, he headed back up to the house with Bullet darting to and fro through the dry brush, chasing his ball. Eli thought he might drop in on Alexis and see if she needed a hand serving the food.

In truth, he was hoping to get a few moments alone with Alexis. He needed some guidance, and Alexis was the logical one to give it to him. She might be a little overanimated at times, and had been known to be a bit of a gossip around town, but she was also something of a matchmaker, and he knew she would never betray a confidence between friends. They'd known each other for years, and right now he could really use a friend's input. He'd have to be fast, though, to make sure he had a chance to speak his piece, before they were interrupted. The last thing he wanted was for Mary to overhear him requesting advice on how to ask her out! Especially since he wasn't at all certain how Alexis would respond to the news that he was interested in his trainer.

That Alexis counted Mary among her closest friends would either help him or hurt him. If she didn't turn all mama tiger on him, trying to protect Mary from a man who was a known failure in the romance department, maybe she could help him figure out what to do. He knew he was attracted to Mary, and he wanted to get to know her better, but he wasn't positive his heart was ready for another roller coaster ride.

He'd been so completely devastated when Natalie had walked out on him. Now, though, when he thought about the life he would have had with her—always trying to please her and never living up to her expectations—he felt more relief than heartbreak. Natalie didn't know it, but she had saved Eli from making a terrible mistake that he would have regretted for the rest of his life. But even though he was glad the wedding had never taken place, the whole disaster had still had a lasting impact on his confidence. He was more cautious now, less willing to trust—especially when it came to his heart.

Was it fair to Mary to ask her to take a chance on a man who still wasn't truly whole? Could he ask her to take a chance on a relationship he wasn't sure he was ready to handle? He hated the thought of losing his shot to win someone as special as Mary…but he wouldn't be able to live with himself if he dove into a relationship too soon and ended up hurting her.

And that was why he needed guidance.

"Can I help you set the table or anything?" he asked Alexis as he came through the back door. It didn't even occur to him to knock first to announce his presence.

Alexis was standing in front of the oven stirring something in an iron skillet. She was dancing in place and humming along to what must have been a peppy tune playing through the headphones from her MP3 player. She was completely unaware of his presence, and when he touched her shoulder, she swung around with a start, nearly hitting him with her spatula. The iron skillet she'd been holding clattered back onto the stovetop.

She laid a hand to her heart. "My word, Eli. You frightened me half to death. I didn't hear you come in."

"I can see that. You were completely lost in whatever music you were listening to."

"How do you know it was music? I could have been listening to an audiobook to stretch and improve my mind."

"You were dancing," he reminded her. "And humming."

"I guess it's a good thing you came by, then,

isn't it? I might have danced off into the sunset and burned the potatoes."

"Mmm. Country-fried potatoes. My favorite."

"I thought T-bone steaks were your favorite. You're welcome to stay for supper, if you'd like."

"Country-fried is my favorite way to eat potatoes," he clarified. "And thank you for the invite, but I've got a few things I need to take care of at home." Could he bring up Mary now? No, it would be too awkward to throw it into the conversation. Reaching for something else to talk about, he said, "I'm glad I came today. Bullet liked showing off for the teenagers, but he certainly got dusty doing it. He's going to need a serious bath, or he's gonna trail dirt all over my nice, clean apartment."

The dog whined and cocked his head when he heard his name.

Alexis chuckled. "And you are going to stand there and try to tell me that you were showing off for the teenagers only?"

Here was his opening to bring up his feelings for Mary…but he couldn't bring himself to take it. He was too busy blushing. Good thing he had whiskers to cover it. He nodded, as if he didn't comprehend her meaning.

She didn't push him. "You can set the silverware, if you really want to help." She pointed to the drawer and then at the long, rectangular table with benches for seating.

Eli counted the place settings and grabbed the appropriate number of forks, butter knives and spoons, then divided them with a set next to each plate.

"Fork has four letters, like left," Alexis reminded him. "Knife and spoon have five, like right."

"Huh," he said, scratching his chin as he surveyed his incorrect place settings. "That's clever. I've never heard that before. I've always arranged them—however." He gestured vaguely at the tabletop.

"It seems like you've been learning a lot lately."

Humph. Some segue. And while he was relieved that she'd brought up the subject herself, he couldn't help but be amused at the awkward transition.

"Mary has brought you and Bullet quite a long way, hasn't she? I was pretty impressed by the show you put on for the *kids*," she said, slightly emphasizing the last word. Clearly Alexis was on to him.

Eli chuckled, then cringed when he realized how nervous he sounded. "Thank you. It hasn't been easy—for Mary, I mean. I'm not always the most cooperative student."

"So she says."

His gut clenched. "She's talking about me?" *And saying bad things?*

He didn't ask the second question aloud.

"Only to Samantha and me, and we don't count. We share everything in our lives, good and bad."

Eli wanted to duck and cover, maybe plunge under the table and pull the cloth over him. That *bad* was what he was concerned about. Maybe he shouldn't follow through on his feelings after all.

"Don't worry. It's mostly good, I promise," she continued, as if she'd guessed his thoughts.

"Well, that's a relief," he drawled, striving toward cavalier and landing somewhere near cynical. "I'd hate to think she was speaking poorly of me."

"Are you kidding me? How could she even think poorly of you when she—" Alexis's declaration came to a screeching halt.

"When she—what?" Eli prodded, intrigued by Alexis's slip of the tongue.

Alexis waved a hand and turned back to the stove, stirring the potatoes with abandon. "Nothing. Forget I said anything."

"No." Eli reached for her elbow and turned

her to face him. "I want to know. I need to hear what you were about to say."

Alexis sighed, then raised her spatula and shook it under Eli's nose. "If you hurt her, Elijah Bishop, you're going to answer to me, and it isn't going to be pretty."

"I don't want to upset her, Alexis," he assured her, his voice dropping deep into his throat. "You know me better than that."

"I don't think you'd wound her on purpose. But Mary has an extra-tender and sensitive heart. Don't toy with her if you don't mean it."

Eli lowered his brows over his eyes. His pulse was pounding in his ears, half in denial, half in hope. How had they gotten into this conversation in the first place? Was she saying what it sounded like she was saying, or was he reading his own emotions into it?

"I'd never toy with her. I really do feel something for her. I'm just not sure I'm ready for... I mean, do you think it's too soon? For her and for me, after everything that happened?"

"Maybe it's too soon, maybe not. Because..." She glanced down at the skillet and then back at Eli. "Have you ever considered that maybe you chose the wrong sister?"

Considered it? Mary had been the only thing on his mind since the day she had sprained her ankle, and he'd had to carry her back to her vehicle. Mary's sweet scent. Mary's determination to make her dreams a reality. Mary's tender, caring heart that never passed over an animal in need—or a human, either. But wishing he'd fallen for her from the start couldn't change what had happened with Natalie.

"It…occurred to me," he admitted vaguely.

Alexis laid a hand on his arm and met his eyes with a deep, penetrating gaze that set him squirming.

"As far as I'm concerned, it's never too soon to be with the right person—the one who can make you the happiest. Mary would be good for you, you know," Alexis said, her already rich alto voice lowering to a whisper. "She's nothing like her sister."

"I know," he responded, having issues with his own voice. He couldn't swallow around the lump of emotion clouding his throat, because he *did* know Mary would be good for him, in all the ways Natalie had not been, and then some. The problem was, he wasn't sure he'd be good for her.

"So what are you going to do about it?" Alexis stirred the potatoes, judged them done and turned off the burner.

Eli leaned his shoulder against the refrigerator door and countered her question with one of his own. "What do you think I should do about it?"

"For starters, I'd say be honest with her. Let her know what you're afraid of, so that you can work through it together."

Work through it together? Share his fears? Not a chance. Hadn't his pride taken enough of a beating with the canine training? Mary had already seen too many of his inadequacies— how could he expect her to want to be with him if he revealed even more?

"Maybe," he hedged. "Eventually. But what else can I do for now, to see if having a relationship with me is something she'd even consider?"

She was silent for a moment, tapping her index finger against her lips.

"I'd say you should take your time, take things slow. That would be the most comfortable for both of you. Start with something small, and low pressure. The Sweetheart Social," she pronounced definitively. "Valentine's Day is next week. It will be the perfect opportunity for you to—"

Her sentence ended abruptly and she pulled away from Eli as if he'd caught on fire. Startled, Eli looked in the direction of Alexis's wide-eyed gaze to find Mary standing just inside the back doorway, white as a sheet, with an unreadable expression on her face, and her lips pinched into a tight line.

How long had she been standing there? How much of their conversation had she heard?

What had Alexis been about to say when they'd been interrupted? And what exactly did she think he ought to say or do at the town's Sweetheart Social?

Chapter Six

Mary's heart jumped into her throat and then plunged into her belly, where it churned like a garden tiller plowing untidy rows in the pit of her stomach.

She'd considered—she'd suspected—that there might be a spark of something between Eli and Alexis, but knowing it in her head and seeing it with her eyes were two entirely different things. Finding Eli and Alexis huddled together gazing at each other and whispering in hushed tones was almost more than Mary could bear.

Add to that the fact that both of them had bolted away from each other when they'd realized she'd entered the room—well, it didn't take a rocket scientist to figure out there was something going on between them.

Of course there was. There was no reason Eli

and Alexis would not be attracted to each other. Pretty is as pretty does, and both of them were highly qualified in that category.

And then there was Mary.

"I beg your pardon," she said, stepping forward. The moment where she possibly could have slinked away without being discovered was long past her. She'd already managed to destroy whatever intimacy was going on between her two friends, so she might as well join them. "I didn't mean to interrupt your private conversation. I can go, if you'd like."

"Oh, nonsense," Alexis exclaimed, laughing a bit more boisterously than the occasion called for. "You weren't interrupting anything. Eli and I were just…"

Yeah. Mary knew exactly what Alexis and Eli were *just* doing. She wished she could crawl into a hole in the floor, and escape this awkward and painful situation completely.

"I was setting the table," Eli offered, opening the silverware drawer and reaching for some serving spoons. "How many did you say you needed, Alexis?"

Alexis turned back to the stove and poured her skillet of potatoes into a large decorative blue bowl. "Five ought to do it. Are you staying for supper, Mary?"

"No, I…have things to do."

Alexis chuckled. "Funny. That's what Eli said when I asked him."

"Oh." Mary couldn't come up with a single clever response. Her mind was simply…scattered, and her heart was plainly wounded.

"You wouldn't happen to have that box of stuff for Bullet, would you?" Eli asked. "The crazy dog is always hungry. I can't believe he's already eaten through the big bag of kibble you gave me."

"That's a K-9 for you. They work hard, play hard and eat hard."

Eli grinned. "That's for sure. So you have it with you? Great! I can walk you out and switch the bundle over to my vehicle. I brought the truck because I can't figure out how to fit Bullet on my motorbike. If I ever do, though, we two will look *awesome* together." He fisted his hands in front of him like he was revving the engine on his bike.

The image of Bullet balancing on the back of Eli's motorcycle as they sped down the road made Mary smile—a little. It also made her want to cry.

"I'm afraid I gave you the wrong impression," Mary replied. He must think she was every kind of scatterbrained. "Bullet's supplies are at my house."

"No problem. I can swing by your place and pick it up now, if you'd like."

"I don't want you to go out of your way on my account. Will you be home tonight? I can drop it off in, say, an hour?" Talk about jumping right out of the frying pan and into the fire.

"All right. If you're sure it's not too much trouble for you. I'd say we could wait on it, if it wasn't for the whole out-of-kibble issue."

"It's not a problem, I promise. In any case, I wouldn't want Bullet to go hungry. Poor thing."

"An hour, then."

An hour. One single hour for her to wrap her mind around the fact that Alexis and Eli were actually becoming a couple. It would be easier if she disliked one or the other of them, but in truth she wanted the best for each of them.

The hard part would be coming to terms with the idea that what was best for both of them might be each other.

And that left Mary as she had been and probably always would be…

Alone.

Eli surveyed his apartment as he waited for Mary to arrive, feeling peculiarly antsy and unable to focus. This was one time he wished he wasn't quite so close to being OCD. It would have been nice to have magazines on his coffee table to straighten or clothes to snatch off the floor in his bedroom. But there were no magazines, and his clothes were all neatly organized and put away in his drawers and closet.

For the first time in his life, he looked at his apartment with new eyes—perhaps as Mary would see it. And it was...

Empty.

Like his life felt right now. Stark. Bleak. Formal.

Sterile.

And while he found Mary's house to be one doggy chew away from utter chaos, at least her house was a *home*—lived-in and noisy.

Alive.

Maybe it was worth the risk to let someone in, to risk being vulnerable, if it made his life feel as warm and vibrant as Mary's smile.

Technically she was a single person living alone, as was he, but at least she had all of her dogs for companionship. Now that Bullet had taken up residence with him, he realized that that counted for something. And while he wasn't ever completely at ease in Bullet's company, he found himself having one-way conversations with the dog—out loud. Maybe he was crazy. Or maybe it was something else altogether.

Him a dog person? Now wouldn't that just beat all?

"You're gonna be on your best behavior when Mary gets here, right, buddy?" he asked Bullet, who was comfortably ensconced in the middle of the floor on his overstuffed bright yellow pillow. He was busy chomping away on a rawhide bone Eli had offered him as a treat, but he looked up when Eli spoke to him. He tilted his head, wagged his tail once and promptly redirected his attention to his bone.

Eli sniffed. "I'll take that as a yes. We've got to impress the pretty lady because…"

Why?

And he would say…

What?

Oops, I accidentally and foolishly chose the wrong sister to propose to. I'm over her, but I'm still an emotional wreck. Will you go out with me?

Then he could mention that he hated dogs and she loved them, but he was sure they could work through their differences. That opposites must attract, because he couldn't get her out of his mind. How many ways would she find to say *brainless?*

Maybe he shouldn't rush into asking her out yet. There was still time, right? At least he got to work with her on a daily basis, for now. He didn't even want to think about when his training would be finished. He never wanted to graduate from her course. He looked forward to getting up each morning, to spending time with her, learning more about her with every day that passed.

And then there was the town's Sweetheart Social coming up on Friday, where he would have the opportunity to—do whatever Alexis was about to suggest when Mary had interrupted them, if he could even figure out what that was.

He didn't have time to work up any kind of plan for the social, because at that moment, Mary buzzed the intercom for him to let her into the apartment complex.

"Did you decorate the place yourself?" she asked as he took a large box of dog paraphernalia from her arms and placed it on the island that separated the kitchen from the living area.

"Yes, if you can call it that," he admitted, scrubbing a hand along his jaw and suddenly wishing he'd put more thought and effort into his decor, such as it was.

"Amazing."

"What?" That was so far from the response Eli was expecting from her that he was sure his mouth was gaping.

"Seriously. It's so clean and edgy, like something out of a high-end home decorating magazine. One theme. Matching pieces. All the furniture carefully placed. And I love that you have pictures of your family on your wall. Perfect. Classy."

Eli's chest welled with pride and gratitude, and he couldn't help but stand a little taller at Mary's praise.

"Versus my house," she continued with a groan. "Utter chaos. You must think I'm one of those hoarders, living in an utter pigpen."

Eli was taken aback. He *had* been thinking of her house as chaotic, but he'd been thinking of the benefits, not the detriments. He was beginning to see the advantages of the frenzy that accompanied the bedlam.

It was lived-in. It was Mary. And he liked it.

She'd seen and accentuated the positive in his bleak excuse for an apartment. He wished he could find the words to compliment hers, but he had nothing.

"Do you want a cup of coffee?" he offered. Could he be any more inept at saying what he felt? More proof that he was right to ignore Alexis's advice about sharing his fears. If he couldn't even muster up a compliment, how could he manage to talk about his insecurities without sounding like an idiot?

"Yes, please. Black." She'd taken his curve in the conversation with remarkable ease, but then, that was Mary.

He moved into the kitchen and poured two mugs of coffee. He took his with milk and more spoonfuls of sugar than he probably should.

"I brought along a dog bed and also some toys for Bullet to play with," she said, gesturing to the fluffy yellow pillow where Bullet lay contentedly munching on his rawhide, "but I see that you've already anticipated many of his long-term needs."

Eli snorted. "If you don't count feeding the poor pup. I failed to foresee Bullet's never-ending hunger. I underestimated the needs and overkilled on the wants, his beds and toys."

She lifted a brow. Her green eyes were alive, glittering in the low light of the nearby standing lamp. "How is that, exactly?"

"That cushion there is not his only bed. He has one in my bedroom, as well, although I crate him at night like you taught me to."

"Trust me. That's best for both of you. Otherwise the first time you doze off in bed, Bullet will sneak up and join you. He knows a good thing when he sees one, and he'll take advantage every chance he gets. And for the record, dogs are major bed-hogs."

Eli couldn't contain the shiver that rocked him to his very core. His imagination immediately went into overdrive.

Why did this keep happening?

He was doing better with his phobia. He *was*. Most of the time. But then he'd experience a moment like this when, despite his best efforts and defenses, his mind would flash back to that field, that dog, that moment of not knowing if he was going to live or die, but knowing for certain it was completely out of his control.

He bit the inside of his lip until he tasted copper.

"Is the dog food in the back of your SUV? If you give me a minute and your car keys, I will run down and grab the kibble." And make a clean escape.

"It's not locked. And thank you. I wasn't looking forward to carrying two forty-pound bags of dog food up two flights of stairs."

Eli scoffed. "As if I'd ever let you do such a thing. You're not going to be hauling around heavy kibble while I'm around to say anything about it." He'd meant it to come out as a gentlemanly statement but feared he'd sounded chauvinistic, or at the very least, egotistical.

"I appreciate the thought—and the action," she said softly, making him feel like that much more of a man just because of her gaze.

She shifted, laying her fingers over her neck. Eli's gaze followed the gesture and noted how quickly her pulse was beating. He swallowed hard.

"If you want to play with Bullet while I'm gone, I've purchased a few toys for him." He opened the coat closet and gestured to the contents. The word *few* might have been a bit of an understatement. He'd had to put in shelves. There were three rows of plastic bins on the shelf, labeled with their contents, everything from rawhide bones to squeaky toys. Toby, the tennis ball, had a place of honor in a small bin of his own.

Eli left Mary to her own devices while he carried up the two bags of kibble, one in each arm, trying without success *not* to analyze the situation in front of him. He was usually fairly proficient at ignoring his feelings, but these just wouldn't go away. They nagged him and nagged him, and he didn't have any idea what to do with them.

"I don't know whether to be impressed by your closet or appalled by it," she said as he rejoined her.

"I beg your pardon?"

"Binned and labeled," she explained with an astonished sniff. "It goes beyond comprehension."

"Guilty as charged. What can I say? I like playing with my label maker."

"I can see that. You are outshining me in

every regard today. I have dog toys and tennis balls spread all over my house."

Eli chuckled. "I know."

Mary's face colored a pretty shade of rose. He loved that he could do that to her—keep her off balance. Make her blush. Cause her pretty green eyes to glitter like emeralds.

"I'm the hopeless housekeeper, while you are—"

"Mr. Neat Freak," he finished for her.

"I wasn't going to say *freak,* but if the shoe fits…"

"You have no idea."

"You are probably a morning person, too."

He didn't know what that had to do with anything, and somehow she made it sound like an insult.

"Let me guess," she continued. "Six a.m.? Seven?"

"Close." He was starting to figure out where the conversation was going. Although Mary was teasing him with her challenges, she was also highlighting yet more respects in which the two of them were polar opposites. He hated even to answer her, but he did. "I'm up by four-thirty, most mornings, so I have time for a run before work."

"Ugh." She gave a mock shiver and cupped her mug of coffee in both hands. "Nothing, not even a fire in my house, would entice me to get up that early in the morning. It's all I can do to be ready for work at eight. Catch me in the evening, though, and I'm ready to rumble."

Eli shook his head. Why were they even talking about sleep cycles? He didn't want to think about all the differences that existed between them. He'd rather focus on what they shared in common.

"Valentine's Day is coming up on Friday. I think the church ladies are making the Sweetheart Social an especially big deal this year, what with all the single adults in town." Now *there* was a smooth segue. He had just dived off a cliff headfirst without even knowing if there was water underneath him, much less how deep it was.

His statement could hardly be viewed as casual, especially since he had blurted it out of nowhere. Now would be a good time for the earth to open up and swallow him whole.

Mary didn't comment. Instead, she set her coffee aside, knelt and buried her face in Bullet's fur.

Fear coursed like lightning through Eli's veins. It was his stupid phobia again, acting in overdrive. His first instinct was to drag her away from the dog—the potential threat—

before his nightmare was reenacted right before his eyes, to a woman he cared deeply for.

He averted his gaze and took a deep breath, praying this fear would disappear and never return. Instead, his past played before his eyes.

He was four, doing what four-year-olds did, playing hide-and-seek with his older brother and sister in a field behind their house. He'd found the perfect place to hide, near an overgrown tree stump that looked as if it had been there forever, its once stately form now reduced into shriveled, hooked branches.

He'd started fidgeting as the shadows engulfed him. He didn't like the shadows. They scared him. The place was far too spooky for him to stay hidden for long. He had just decided to reveal himself to his siblings and receive their ridicule when suddenly a wolf hybrid sprang from a dark burrow Eli hadn't even noticed existed at the base of the stump.

Eli hadn't a chance to react before the animal was on top of him. He was dimly aware of claws and fur and teeth, as he sank to the ground and rolled into a ball to protect his face.

Vee had challenged the dog with a big stick and scared her off into the brush. They discovered later that she'd been protecting her pups, but by then it was too late for Eli to rationalize the attack. His fears were as permanent as the tooth-and-claw scars across his forearm and shoulder, a constant reminder of the incident and of the dangers of letting himself be vulnerable.

"Eli?" Mary's sweet voice slowly penetrated the fog of his reverie. He felt as if he'd been wakened from a dead sleep, a deep dream state. His mind was hazy, and his thought process was moving at a snail's pace.

"I lost you there for a minute," she continued. "Where did you go just now?" She remained crouched by Bullet, her arm loosely draped around his neck, not appearing to mind the way the dog lapped at her cheek.

Eli shook his head. "I didn't go anyplace," he denied, perhaps a little more forcefully than he should have.

Except to revisit the past I'd rather forget.

"It's… Well, you looked…" Mary stammered, then let her sentence drop.

The intercom to his apartment buzzed into the nervous silence, causing them both to jump. Eli had never heard a more welcome sound in his life.

"Were you expecting someone?" Mary asked.

"No, I don't think so." He glanced at his watch, wondering if he might have forgotten some kind of important meeting.

In three long strides he reached the intercom

receiver and pushed the incoming button. "Yes? Who is it, please?"

"It's me, little brother, and I've brought your favorite cookies. Count your blessings that you have a sister as nice as me. I stopped by Cup O' Jo's Café, and Phoebe was baking peanut butter cookies, so of course I thought of you."

Eli hadn't been expecting his sister this evening, but his family members were always welcome and often dropped in unannounced.

"You're going to be all cookied-out," Mary told him, punctuated by a strained chuckle.

"Me? Never." He patted his belly for emphasis. "Always room for another cookie, I say. Especially the ones Phoebe Hawkins bakes."

"I have to avoid Cup O' Jo's or I'll cheat on my diet for sure," she admitted. Her eyes widened, looking terrified, as if she'd encountered a big spider or something. Eli looked at the wall behind him but saw nothing that would alarm her. By the time he'd turned back, her attention was on Bullet again. She scratched him behind the ears and talked to him in a soothing voice.

Eli felt as if she were withdrawing herself from him. Had he said something to cause her distress? He didn't think he had. They'd been talking about cookies, for pity's sake. He hadn't a clue what he'd done, or what he should do now. And he didn't have time to ponder it further before his sister, Vee, came bursting through the door.

"Like I was telling you, I smelled fresh peanut butter cookies when I was on my way home, and I haven't seen you for a couple of weeks, so I thought—"

Her sentence came to an abrupt halt when she spied Mary crouching on the floor next to Bullet.

"Oooh," she said, drawing out the word as if she'd had a sudden burst of insight. "I'm sorry. I didn't realize you had *company.*"

Eli cringed, feeling embarrassed more for Mary than for himself. There was no doubt from Vee's tone that she was making a big deal about the fact that her brother was entertaining *female* company. Vee was reading a great deal more into that scenario than what really existed. As for Eli, he had no problem associating himself with Mary, but he had no idea how she felt about it.

She bounded to her feet so fast that she almost tripped over the dog.

"I was just leaving. I only stopped by to drop off a couple bags of kibble for Bullet."

Well, that clinched it. She didn't want his sister to think they were involved.

"You don't have to leave on my account," Vee protested. "I can come back another time. I'm sure my kid brother would much rather spend his time with a pretty woman than with his boring, old sister."

Vee couldn't have delivered the tongue-in-cheek line any smoother, but the color of Mary's face went from bright rose to blanched white in an instant. Eli thought, given the heat burning the tips of his ears, that his own face must be an intense shade of red.

"I… It… I'm not…" Mary stuttered. "I think I'll go now."

She couldn't get out of his apartment fast enough. She practically ran out the door. Eli followed her, but she was already halfway down the stairs by the time he'd reached his door. The hallway echoed with the sound of her feet tramping down the steps in a rapid, uneven staccato.

When he could no longer hear the sound of Mary's feet, he turned back to his sister, who had taken the liberty of pouring herself a cup of coffee.

Vee's eyebrows rose, and her eyes sparkled with mischief. "Do you want to tell me what that was all about, or do I have to guess? Because I guarantee you that anything I come up with is going to be far more embarrassing for you than anything you can dream up."

"You're reading too much into this."

Vee choked on her sip of coffee. "I highly doubt that, little brother."

"Mary was only bringing some things by for me because she is the one with the regrettable honor of trying to teach me how to work in a K-9 unit."

"Poor woman." She leaned her hip against the kitchen counter. "I still don't get why you didn't tell Captain James that you have a problem with dogs."

Eli straightened and set his own mug of coffee on the island counter. "And why would I do that?"

"Uh, maybe because you can't even be in the same room as a dog?" she suggested with the slightest hint of sarcasm. She was his sister, after all. At the word *dog,* Bullet trotted forward and sat in front of Vee. She chuckled and scratched his ears. "You giving my brother a hard time? I don't know, baby brother. I can't imagine why you thought you could work with Bullet day in and day out."

"Well, I am, aren't I?"

"Guess so," Vee admitted grudgingly. "How's that working out for you?"

Eli scoffed and crossed his arms. "How do you think? I hate it. It's pure torture for me."

"Then why not pass it off to another officer?"

"It's a promotion," he said firmly, as much to

himself as to Vee. "And the whole force knows I've accepted the position. I'm not turning it down now. That would just leave everyone to wonder why. They're still giving me guff about Natalie running off before our wedding. I don't need to give the guys anything else they can hold over me, and I certainly don't want to give the ladies in town more fodder for the gossip mill."

"So what are you going to do, then?" Vee tilted her head and regarded him thoughtfully, pulling the clip from her bun and shaking her long dark hair over her shoulders.

Eli still couldn't get used to her wearing it down, the way she now did when she was off duty, ever since the day Ben Atwood had put a ring on her finger. She'd worn it in a bun for so many years before that it was like seeing a new person. A softer, sweeter version of the girl he'd grown up with.

"I'm going to do my job." He cleared his throat.

"And you're okay with that?"

"Mostly." He frowned and shook his head. "I don't want to talk about it."

Vee barked out a laugh. "Of course you don't. But I know how hard it is for you to face down your fears. You aren't giving poor Mary a hard time, are you?"

Heat rose to his face. He hoped his sister couldn't see it, but it was clear from the expression on her face that she'd immediately picked up on his discomfort. As far as he was concerned, talking about Mary was completely off-limits, especially to his perceptive older sister.

"Why, you *are,* you little pickle, you." She jabbed him in the ribs. He might be bigger than her now, but she still treated him like her little brother. "How did you explain to Mary about your—*aversion* to dogs?"

"I haven't. And I'm not going to. She doesn't need to know, any more than the guys on the force do."

Vee's gaze narrowed on him speculatively. She took a slow sip of coffee. "Doesn't she?"

Eli shook his head. He was adamant about this, and nothing Vee could say would change his mind. Mary would never know. *He* certainly wasn't going to tell her. And he wasn't going to let Vee give him away, either.

"Look, I know you don't like to share what happened to you when you were four. I get that. It's personal and private. Believe me, I know all about those two words. But I would think it would be easier for you both if you came clean to Mary. Mary is the sweetest thing. She won't tell anyone about your secret. You have nothing to be ashamed about, Eli. It's just part of your past. If you ask me, it's something you haven't ever really dealt with. Maybe being placed in this K-9 unit is God's way of helping you get over your pain."

"You think?" Eli was not entirely convinced. No one understood how difficult this was for him, not even his sister. So how could he expect Mary Travis, a dog lover to the core, to understand?

And now his growing feelings for Mary were complicating matters even further. He felt like he was spinning into crazy heights on a Ferris wheel and then swinging low again, and no one was there to release the latch on the door. He'd see the ground in reach and then the wheel would circle back up again.

Stop the ride—he wanted to get off!

"Maybe Mary can help you." Vee was pushing, and he didn't like it.

"I don't want to bring Mary into this," he insisted.

"Why not? I would think that of all people, Mary would be able to — Oooh." There was that know-it-all sound again. Eli was getting really annoyed by it.

"What?" he snapped.

"This is more about Mary than it is about Bullet."

Eli scowled. "How do you figure?"

"You *like* her," she taunted, in the same infuriating voice she'd used a million times when they were children.

"Of course I like her. She's a nice woman."

"Nice? I don't think so. Why didn't you tell me this was what it was really about? I can help you."

He scoffed. "Oh, like you're an expert in matters of the heart. You and Ben had such an easy road when you were getting together, right?"

"You know that's not true, which is what makes me an expert. I made every mistake in the book. I can advise you on the pitfalls, so you can avoid them."

"Sounds ominous," he said, leaning his back against the counter and slouching into his crossed arms.

"But worth it. What's your plan?"

"What plan?"

"I know you, Eli. You're a plotter. You don't go off half-cocked. If you want to get her attention, then you've already come up with a way to do so."

He wished that were true. He was still hanging on to the hope that he'd somehow figure out whatever it was that Alexis had been about to say to him to point him in the right direction. He didn't have a GPS, and he didn't have a map. He didn't even know what country he was in.

Vee was waiting, one eyebrow arched and a knowing smile on her face.

"The Sweetheart Social," he hedged. Maybe Vee would take the ball and run with it, give him some good suggestions without even realizing she was doing so.

"Perfect!" she exclaimed.

"You think?"

"Of course. You show up with flowers and chocolate and proclaim your undying love for her. Sweep her right off her feet. She won't even know what hit her."

Eli snorted. "I don't think so. What's plan B?"

"I thought you would know. You're sure, then? No flowers?"

"I don't know. One, maybe. But even that might be too much for her. I think I need to be subtle, take this slow. She doesn't know I'm interested in her, and I'm not at all sure she's interested in me."

"Okay, then, nix the flowers. You don't want to frighten the poor woman off. Hmm. Let me think." She tapped her chin with her index finger, then held it up like a lightbulb had gone off in her head. "You should bring Bullet."

"And why would I do that? I never get a break from that dog as it is."

"You've got to think about what interests her,

and that would be dogs. Then you play into that. Get her attention. You see?"

"I think I'm starting to." Maybe his sister was right. Mary would be impressed with him if he brought Bullet to the social, wouldn't she? And from there, maybe he could get a moment alone with her. It was worth a try.

"And a tie," Vee declared.

"No way. I don't do ties."

"Not even for Mary?"

"I don't even own one."

"Ben can loan you one for the evening. What color of dress shirt were you planning to wear?"

"How should I know?" Vee pelting him with all these pointless questions was thoroughly exasperating. "Whatever's in my closet, I guess."

"Wear the royal-blue one," she decided for him. "I'll bring you one of Ben's ties to match. You'll be the most handsome guy at the social—other than my Ben, of course."

Handsome, shmandsome. But to get Mary to think of him in a romantic light, he'd do whatever it took—even wear a tie.

Chapter Seven

Biting back the urge to cry, Mary stared at the heart-shaped invitation in her hand. Serendipity's Valentine's Day Sweetheart Social was the next day, and she had already decided she wasn't about to make an appearance. While she typically loved taking part in community events, the Sweetheart Social, with its emphasis on love and romance that just made her feel alone, was the exception to that rule—especially this year, when her whole perspective on her life had changed.

What single woman would want to subject herself to the walking-through-fire trial of a bunch of happily married couples determined to set her poor single self up with this or that man? In their eyes, she couldn't possibly be happy on her own. Which she was—or she had been, until Eli had come back into her life. There was only one man for Mary, and all of her attempts to avoid falling for him—and getting her heart crushed in the end—were failing. At this rate, she wouldn't be able to keep her feelings in check much longer, and then what would she do?

Talk about mixed memories and stir-fried emotions. Whenever she thought of the social, she remembered her very first attendance, in the ninth grade— and most of all, despite her best efforts to the contrary, she remembered Eli.

He'd been a senior then, the star running back on the football team, the guy every boy wanted to be and all the girls—Mary included—wanted to date.

Samantha and Alexis, both outgoing and well liked themselves, each had brought dates of their own, and while they tried to include her, there was only so much they could do without appearing rude to the guys who'd brought them. She might as well have borrowed from Jo Spencer's wacky T-shirt collection, always on display when Jo was working at her shop, Cup O' Jo's Café, and worn one that read Third Wheel.

Young and plain and awkward, she'd slipped into the shadow of one of the cement pillars and watched the multigenerational fun from a distance. Laughing, eating, singing, dancing

It seemed everyone was in the party spirit. Everyone except her.

And then Eli had approached, gently tapping her shoulder and asking if she'd be his partner in a country reel.

He'd laughed, and she'd laughed as he spun her around, not so much an expert in his execution as he was simply filled with the joy of the moment, and it rubbed off on her. Afterward he'd gotten her a glass of lemonade and had politely deposited her right back where he'd found her. Other boys had asked her to dance after that, but she knew it was only because Eli had noticed her first.

And she'd loved him for it. Even now, her heart welled when she thought of the kindness the popular teen had showed one lonely misfit.

As her high school years passed, and her friendship with Samantha and Alexis broadened, she had become less of a social outcast and more of a public expert, and town gatherings had become less painful for her. Even the affable moniker for their little trio—the Little Chicks, due to the way they cheeped and chattered when they were together—helped her adjust.

But now she was back to facing a social gathering with the kind of anguish and awkwardness she had not felt in years—or ever, really.

Mary could not think of one thing on earth that would be more tormenting than to watch Eli fall in love with yet another woman, even if that woman was one of her best friends.

Mary balled the invitation into her fist and sighed distraughtly. With an overhand toss, the once heart-shaped piece was firmly ensconced in the trash bin at the end of her desk. Her office was currently in the back corner of her living room. She'd eventually need new space, now that she was officially launching her kennel business. Paperwork was piling up around her ears, especially with the added burden of the police reports. Her living room appeared messy enough without the added clutter. She certainly didn't need a makeshift office to make it any worse.

Come to think of it, addressing the eons of paperwork added to her by the police department was as good an excuse as any for not attending this event. That should be enough to put people off without having to admit the simple truth.

Happy people and a hurting heart didn't mix.

She gave a start when the front doorbell rang. She stood from her cheap desk chair and stretched the small of her back, then glanced at her watch.

Eight-thirty p.m. Eli had left hours ago, and she wasn't expecting any other company.

Samantha and Alexis burst in the door as soon as she opened it, their voices garbled as they strove to speak over each other. As always, they excelled in their exuberance. Mary could well understand how they'd been dubbed the Little Chicks in high school. She only shared the moniker because she always hung around them. There was a rare synthesis of energy when the three of them were in one room together, although admittedly it mostly came from her two lively friends.

"Did you get your invitation? Isn't it pretty this year? Do you have a date? What are you going to wear? I was thinking red—do you think that color might wash out my complexion too much?"

Mary's mood shifted. She laughed and held her hands up, palms outward. She couldn't remain sober in spirit for long with these ladies around.

"Slow down, girls. One question at a time, from one person at a time. I'm in serious sensory overload right now."

In more ways than one.

Alexis spotted the crumpled invitation and fished it out of the tiny trash can in the corner.

"Now, what is this?" she demanded, shaking the paper heart under Mary's nose.

"I should think that would be obvious. Didn't you get one?" Mary responded blithely.

"I *know* what it is," Alexis said with an exasperated sigh. "Do you want to explain to me why it's all crinkled up in your trash can?"

"Not particularly." *Especially not to Alexis.* Mary made a face.

Not only would it be awkward for everybody involved, but if Mary told Alexis the true reason she'd destroyed the invitation, that would put a definite crimp in her friend's developing relationship with Eli. No matter how Mary felt about it personally, that was something she would not and could not do to dear Alexis. And Eli was carrying around enough guilt, thanks to Natalie, for Mary to want to add to his burden.

But she had to give the ladies some kind of an explanation for why she was not attending the event. She knew she'd had an excuse only a minute ago...but she couldn't seem to recall it. Under pressure, she scanned her brain for possibilities and came up blank.

In the end she shrugged.

"That's all we're going to get?" Samantha chuckled. "You know and I know that's not good enough."

"You can see all the paperwork I've got piling

up," she said in a sudden flash of remembrance, gesturing to her desk. "The police department demands a paper trail a mile long. I'm finding it difficult to keep up with it all by myself. I thought I could spend Friday night catching up."

Alexis propped her hands on her hips, looking for all the world like a mother about to reprimand her child.

"What?" Mary squeaked.

"If you're that far behind, hire an administrative assistant," Alexis said. "You're an official business now. You can hire employees. In any case, I don't buy it. Something else is going on. Do you believe her, Samantha?"

Samantha shook her head. Fat lot of help she was being. They were ganging up on her, just as she'd been afraid they would. "Nope. Not for a second. It's us, Mary. Spill it. What's really happening here?"

She couldn't reveal what was really happening without hurting someone she cared for. Which only left her with one option.

"All right, you two. You win. I can't fight the both of you. I'll go to the social."

Alexis whooped in delight, and Samantha clapped her hands.

"You have to promise you'll dance—at least once," Alexis prodded, taking advantage of her triumph.

The skin on the back of Mary's neck prickled. "Why is my social life—or in this case, my pathetic lack of one—all of a sudden so important?"

Samantha beamed. "I'm so overwhelmingly happy with my life right now. Will and his daughter fill up my heart and make me complete. Is it any wonder that I want the same thing for you?"

"Okay, I'll buy that," Mary reluctantly agreed. "From you. Even if I don't happen to agree with you. I'm perfectly content working on my new business and spending my time training my dogs. I'm obviously up to my ears in kennel work. The last thing I need is to try to add a man to the mix. I can picture it now. Utter chaos, collapsing all around me."

That was the truth, wasn't it? So why did her mind persist in picturing Eli by her side, bringing order instead of adding to the chaos?

"You don't know until you try," Samantha goaded.

"I cannot imagine what makes you think this particular social function is going to spur on the Big Romantic Change in my life."

"Because it's time," Alexis insisted. "I just feel it."

Mary suspected Alexis felt that way because it was *her* time. It was hard not to be jealous.

"And it's Valentine's Day," Alexis added. "All the singles in town have their hearts set on meeting that special someone. It's traditional."

"Oh, that's rich, coming from you," Mary pointed out. "I don't see a ring on your finger. Are you on the hunt for a man?"

Mary wanted to kick herself. She wished she could take her words back, unask the question. It was rude, and she didn't want to know the answer, anyway.

"Maybe I am," Alexis said slyly, her eyes gleaming.

Was she thinking of Eli?

"I did mention the possibility of wearing red, the color of love. You ought to start thinking about your wardrobe. Better yet, let Samantha and me choose for you."

"I wasn't aware that the color of our clothing was sending messages. I can't imagine the guys are too in tune to that sort of thing, at least not the ones I know."

"Of course not," Alexis agreed with a hearty laugh. "That part is for us girls to know, and the guys to figure out. Now tell me—what are you planning to wear for the social?"

The pink cable-knit sweater Mary's friends had picked out for her was hot and scratchy, and it was making her perspire. That the community center was full to overflowing with every-one from the town octogenarians to the giggly teenagers staying at Redemption Ranch only made it worse. The air was so stuffy that Mary couldn't breathe.

As if that wasn't bad enough, she was alone in the crowd, holed up in the shadow of the same concrete pillar that had been her friend all those years ago at her first social. The entire scenario felt oddly familiar, and she didn't like it one bit.

Thanks to Alexis and Samantha talking her into leaving her glasses at home, she also couldn't *see*. Her friends were, of course, no-where to be found, at least as far as she could tell. Everything was blurry, her stomach was churning, and she felt just as awkward as she had back in high school.

Vanity, meet misery.

Well, as long as she didn't move away from the pillar, she wasn't likely to run into or over anyone, so there was that, at least. She would simply stay in the shadows and maintain a low profile—and hopefully some semblance of her dignity, if God was gracious. She was thirsty, but she wasn't about to chance the dessert and beverage table on her own. She'd probably knock over the whole thing and go straight from awkward to mortified.

She wished for the tenth time in as many minutes that she'd just stayed at home, and not allowed Samantha and Alexis to talk her into something she knew was going to be a total disaster. Since it was their fault she was here, the least they could do was show up to lead around their blind friend, especially since the whole stupid leave-your-glasses-at-home idea was theirs to begin with.

The fiddler began warming up and squares started forming. Mary heard high, familiar laughter and squinted toward the middle of the room, where folks had cleared the way for a makeshift dance floor.

Sure enough, there was Alexis, on the arm of—*Eli*. Of course she was.

Mary inhaled sharply. Why did it feel like a punch in the gut every time she saw the two of them together? It wasn't as if she hadn't anticipated as much. But it wasn't getting any better with time, not like it should be. If anything, it was worse.

She bit her lip to keep her emotions in check and watched as Eli leaned toward Alexis to say something close to her ear. She squealed and swatted at Eli's chest. Mary cringed. Flirting, for Alexis, was as easy as reciting the alphabet.

"A. B. C," Mary whispered under her breath, trying to calm her nerves.

Suddenly she was embraced from behind.

"Where have you been?" Samantha demanded, her husband, Will, and his five-year-old daughter, Genevieve, at her heels. "I've been looking all over for you."

"Then you haven't been looking very hard. I've been standing here for at least a quarter of an hour."

"Well, you can't blame me for that, then. How am I supposed to find you, if you're hiding in the shadows? Why aren't you out on the dance floor? You promised Alexis you'd dance, remember?"

Because the only man I want to dance with is already out there—with Alexis.

"I remember. No one has asked," Mary informed her. "Besides, I can't see to dance because two certain someones convinced me to leave my glasses at home."

"But your eyes are so pretty when you're not hiding them behind those awful glasses. You should get contacts."

"Samantha," Will cautioned, sounding appalled. He edged forward. "Mary, I am so sorry for the way my wife is acting right now. There is obviously something wrong with the wiring between her brain and her mouth."

"I like my glasses, thank you very much," Mary retorted, though she wasn't really offended. She knew her friend's suggestion was harmless and made in love. And it wasn't as if she hadn't heard it before.

"I know you do, honey," Samantha agreed. "Keep your glasses if you want. Now as I recall, you promised Alexis that you'd dance tonight."

"You said that already," Will reminded her, laying a hand on her shoulder. "It's not polite to push."

"It is when I'm her best friend." She elbowed Will. "Soldier boy here can be your first partner, to get things going."

Mary's face flushed as Will shifted, clearly uncomfortable with the less-than-brilliant idea his wife had just offered. He was a wonderful husband to Samantha and a great father to Genevieve, but the former soldier was also a quiet, reserved man, not the touchy-feely type who would want to be dancing with anyone besides his wife. But he also wasn't one to back down from his duty—even if it was a duty his wife had assigned to him without his consent.

Will cleared his throat and held out his hand to Mary.

"Nonsense," Mary chided, quick to turn away that notion. "I'm quite certain Alexis didn't have a married man in mind when she ordered me to dance with someone. And I'll guess you two haven't yet hit the dance floor together tonight.

There's another square forming right now. How about if I watch Genevieve for you while you two take a spin?"

Will flashed her a relieved smile as he turned his attention to his wife. Samantha looked torn, but after a moment she took Will's hand.

"All right, but as soon as we get back, Alexis and I are going to find you an eligible man to dance with."

It wasn't a threat so much as it was a promise. Mary sighed. Maybe the best thing for her to do would be to grit her teeth through a dance with one of them and then make a clean getaway before her friends could embarrass her any further. But who would be the unlucky man?

Mary crouched to Genevieve's level and leaned in close so the little girl could hear her over the blare of the live band.

"Do you want a cupcake?"

Genevieve's eyes widened noticeably and she nodded.

Mary allowed the little girl to lead her to the dessert table, all the while surreptitiously combing the area with her squinty gaze, taking account of all the age-appropriate single men in the room.

Not much to choose from, in Mary's opinion, and certainly nobody new or interesting. Then again, if she was being honest with herself, not a one of them had ever met up to the standard she'd set in Eli.

But she was going to have to pick one of them, if she was ever going to get out of here. Brody and Slade, a couple of hulking bull-riding cops who served on the force with Eli, were roughhousing like a couple of teenagers just past the edge of the beverage table. At their age, Mary thought they ought to be showing at least a modicum of maturity.

There was Pastor Shawn, who was standing along the sidelines of the dance floor, watching the merriment and clapping and stomping his feet to the music—or kind of to the music. He wasn't exactly staying in rhythm. Mary checked him off her list. She wasn't a great dancer to begin with. She needed a man with a strong lead.

What was she going to do?

She would have slipped away right then if she hadn't been taking care of Genevieve. She could hardly leave the five-year-old to her own devices, and so she waited until the music ended, and Samantha and Will returned to her side.

"That cupcake looks yummy, monkey," he said, scooping Genevieve into his arms. "Let's go get your daddy one." The little girl squealed in delight as Will tickled her and then whisked her back to the dessert table.

"That was smooth. Did you tell him to do that?" Mary asked.

"Nope," Samantha replied. "Got him trained. I don't even need to ask."

Mary tried to chuckle, but it came out more like she was choking on a chicken bone. "I wonder if he'd see it that way."

"Excuse me. Pardon me," Alexis crowed, scooting and sashaying through the crowd. "Woman on a mission."

Mary cringed, knowing that she was the mission Alexis had in mind. Now she was going to feel the pressure from two angles. Why hadn't she stayed home?

"Are you ready to burn up the floor?" Alexis asked as she enveloped her in an exuberant hug.

"I highly suspect the only thing that's going to be burning here is my cheeks," Mary murmured under her breath. Louder, she said, "Please tell me you are not planning to embarrass me tonight."

"Of course not."

"We're in this together, then? The two of us single ladies, anyway? I'm not dancing unless you—"

"Sure, sure," Alexis interrupted. "Whatever you want." She locked arms with Mary and turned her toward the crowd. "Now, where is—"

Alexis didn't get to finish whatever it was

she was about to say before the loudspeaker rang from microphone feedback, and everyone groaned and covered their ears.

"Sorry, folks," Jo Spencer apologized from the platform where the band was playing. Her T-shirt of the day was a glaring red, with an enormous pink heart in the center and the words *On the Line* underneath with what looked like a hospital heart monitor zigzag with one beat of the heart a good deal higher than the others.

How completely appropriate, Mary thought. Only in her case, the line was straight, and the pitch of the machine was a frightening monotone.

"I'm not used to using one of these things," Jo continued, setting the microphone aside with a boisterous cackle. "Why bother? I don't need a microphone to be heard, even in a crowd as big as this one."

The crowd in question roared with laughter and clapped for their favorite hostess, a second mother to a good half the town, Mary included. Cup O' Jo's was the place a person went for kudos, consoling or just to talk.

"Now I don't mean to interrupt your celebrating tonight, but I wanted to call your attention to something I think y'all are going to be very interested in. I don't know how many of you know this, but we are honored to have a new

K-9 unit working as part of our wonderful, talented police department."

Mary was sure her jaw hit the floor. What was the crazy woman talking about? Jo didn't know any of the details about the undertaking—as far as Mary knew, it was still meant to be a relatively hush-hush operation until she'd proven she and Eli and Bullet were up to the task. And anyway, the Sweetheart Social was hardly the time and place to make such an announcement.

"Get to it, woman!" Jo's husband, Frank, called from the floor. "Stop priddle-praddling. Some of us want to dance with our wives."

Jo chuckled and shook her finger at him. "Never you mind, Frank. You'll get a dance with your wife when she's good and ready to give you one."

The crowd chuckled and cheered. Poor Frank's impatience was overpowered by the sheer curiosity of folks wanting to know Jo's big reveal.

"Ladies and gents, I'd like to call your attention to our handsome deputy sheriff Eli Bishop and his new partner, Bullet."

The applause was deafening, echoing off the walls of the community center. Eli hopped onto the stage with a flourish with Bullet at his heel.

"Eli and Bullet here have some fancy tricks

to show you. Gather 'round, y'all, and welcome this cute furry critter to our midst."

Apparently Jo had decided that was the end of her public service announcement for the evening, because she waved at the band to strike back up into a lively tune and dragged Frank to the middle of the dance floor, where they were joined by several other couples for a country line dance.

There was still a lot of ruckus going on at the front of the room—high, piercing female laughter and chatter, mostly. *Single* females. It appeared they'd come out of the woodwork to fawn over Eli and Bullet.

Alexis was deep in conversation with Slade McKenna and didn't appear to even notice Eli performing on the other side of the room. Didn't it make her even a little bit jealous? Alexis was clearly a much stronger person than Mary would ever be.

Eli glanced in Mary's direction and caught her eye, and his mouth quirked into a satisfied grin. Her stomach tightened into agonizing knots, and she turned away. She simply could not stand to watch Eli showing off for every unmarried woman between sixteen and sixty.

Anger welled in her chest. This spectacle wasn't what the K-9 unit was about. He was turning all of her time training into a farce.

"I'm sorry," she apologized to her friends. "Being without my glasses has given me a terrible headache." She pressed her fingers to her temple for emphasis. She really did have a headache building, though it had little to do with her absent glasses and everything to do with the increased ringing of female laughter coming from across the room.

"I'm sorry," she said again. "I've got to get out of here."

Now. The air felt thick, and she struggled to breathe.

"You really don't look well," Samantha acknowledged, laying the back of her hand against Mary's forehead. "You feel a little warm. Come on. Will and I'll drive you home."

"Don't be ridiculous," Mary argued weakly. "You two stay and enjoy the social. I can make it home just fine on my own. It's a short walk and the fresh cool air will do me some good."

Alexis looked hesitant. "You're sure you don't want a ride?"

Mary shook her head.

"Text us when you get home. We want to know you are safe. You're absolutely certain you don't want us with you?"

"I'm positive." Mary knew her tone vetoed any misgivings her friends might have had about leaving her to her own devices, and that was a good thing, because that was exactly what she wanted—to be left alone to grieve for what never was, never had been and never would be.

Eli had to admit he hadn't expected quite the positive response he and Bullet had received from the folks in town. He'd been unsure they'd be pleased to hear their taxes were paying for yet another program, even a K-9 unit engaged to keep them safe.

Instead, it kind of felt like people were putting him on a pedestal. He wasn't just a cop— he was a special kind of cop. Suddenly having Bullet as his partner didn't seem quite so awful.

He was glad Jo had insisted on formally introducing him. He'd originally thought it was a bad idea—the wrong place at the wrong time. But he had to admit he enjoyed the attention they'd drawn, and so did Bullet.

Surely Mary had to be pleased with the free publicity he'd given her new business. He'd even managed to squeeze in a clear shout-out so everyone would know Bullet had been specially trained by Mary. People would be knocking down her door to ask her to work their own family pets. She'd have so much business she wouldn't know what to do with it.

Except—where was she?

He'd caught her eye earlier in the evening,

so he knew she had to be somewhere in the community center. Alexis had pulled him aside when he'd first arrived and insisted he dance with her, so she could fill him in on her plan—which apparently was to nonchalantly push him and Mary together. She'd even hinted that Mary had promised to dance with him, which was easily going to be the highlight of his evening. He was here for Mary, and it was a relief to see that he had the backing of her friends. Could a guy ask for more?

He made his apologies to the folks still clamoring for more dog tricks and scanned the room, eager to get the important part of his night started. But again, he didn't see Mary. She wasn't the type of woman to spend hours primping in the ladies' room, thankfully, but at the moment, he couldn't think of where else she could be.

Finally he spied Samantha across the room, standing with Will and Genevieve. He began edging toward her. Alexis was bound to be nearby, and one or the other of them was sure to know where he should look to find Mary.

"Eli," Samantha greeted as he approached and shook hands with Will. "I think Alexis was looking for you earlier."

"She found me. Hey, have either one of you seen Mary? I wanted to know what she thought of the show Bullet and I put on. She ought to be pretty stoked about all the positive response we received for her work."

"She should be," Samantha agreed, "but unfortunately, she wasn't feeling well. I think she has a headache. She decided not to stay."

"She did?" All of Eli's adrenaline and enthusiasm for the evening ahead dropped into the pit of his stomach and rolled like a lead ball. It was bad enough that all of his own plans had flown out the window, but poor Mary! She must be terribly distressed not to be able to enjoy the community party. "How long ago did she leave?"

"I don't know," Samantha said, pulling out her cell phone to check the time. "Five minutes ago? Ten?"

"Was she driving? She probably should have let someone else take her home, if she was feeling ill."

"Alexis and I offered. She blatantly refused. She's on foot—said she thought the fresh air would do her headache good."

"I'll make sure she gets home safely," he vowed, already plunging back into the crowd, heading toward the exit.

"Thank you," Samantha called from behind him. "Please tell her that we love her."

Eli waved back at her, then broke into a jog

the moment he was free of the building. Bullet was running right at his heel. He didn't worry that the dog wouldn't follow him. Bullet was on full alert. Somehow the dog knew how seriously Eli was taking this moment, almost as if he could sense the stress Eli was feeling.

It wasn't until he was passing by the park that he caught his first glimpse of Mary. She was hardly more than a shadow on the dark playground, crouched low on a swing. Only the slight rocking motion clued him in to her presence.

"Mary?" he called when he was within yards of her. "Your friends said you weren't feeling well. What are you doing here?"

Mary sighed. "Go back to the party, Eli. I'm fine."

Ignoring her command, he moved closer.

"I want to make sure you make it home safely. You really should have had someone drive you, given the way you feel."

She frowned and squinted up at him. "I don't need a babysitter. Frankly, I'm tired of people telling me what to do."

He wondered why she wasn't wearing her glasses. He liked those thick black rims. They gave her character and magnified her luminescent green eyes.

It was odd, though. She didn't sound sick.

She sounded *angry*. But what did she have to be angry about?

"I wasn't trying to order you to do anything," he assured her. "I care for you, you know. Don't make my actions into something they're not."

"I'm not making anything out of anything."

Now *there* was a woman's logic if he'd ever heard it. He tilted his head and regarded her closely.

"I still think I ought to walk you home." He paused and pressed his lips together. "I'm asking, not telling, by the way."

"And I'm declining. Politely."

"Your friends would feel better about it if you allowed me to accompany you. They were really worried when you left the way you did."

She scowled and didn't reply.

He might be slow on the uptake, but he was getting the distinct impression she didn't want him around.

Which didn't make a lick of sense. He was here to help her. He would have thought she would appreciate the gesture. He was trying to be a gentleman, after all—to show her that he'd look out for her, take care of her.

Instead of acting pleased or grateful, she seemed—*something*. Irritated? Resentful?

Of what? Him?

This wasn't the way he'd envisioned this evening would turn out at *all*. Granted, he hadn't had much of a plan, other than doing what Vee suggested and bringing Bullet along with him to the party to catch Mary's eye. He'd planned to be careful and take things slow with Mary, but everything had snowballed out of his control. He realized to his dismay that he was no closer to convincing Mary to give him a chance now than he was the first day the Lord had thrown them together for work.

Father, he prayed silently, and a little bit desperately, *You know what Mary needs, even if I don't.*

"I got a lot of compliments on Bullet tonight," he informed her. Maybe if he turned the conversation to their shared interest in the success of the K-9 unit, he could regain some of the footing that he'd obviously lost.

"I'm sure you did," Mary answered bitterly.

"Aren't you happy for me? I would think you'd be excited at the way things went down tonight. The community embraced us."

"You make a mockery of everything I'm trying to do, and you think that's a good thing?" Her voice was low and harsh, from somewhere deep in her throat.

"What? You think that I— How, exactly, did I make a mockery of your work?" he stammered, flabbergasted by her accusation. She was seeing this all wrong. He'd done nothing to hurt her. Every move, both calculated and impulsive, had been for her benefit.

"You weren't showing off? Playing around with *Toby, the tennis ball,* to get a little attention?"

He started to deny the accusation she'd hurled at him but stopped before the words left his lips.

He *had* been showing off—for her. He had been looking for attention—*Mary's* attention. The crowd had been a means to an end.

How was he going to explain that without coming off looking like a fool? It was clear she didn't even like him overmuch right now.

This evening was getting worse by the moment. All of his daydreams, vague as they might have been, melted like butter in the sunshine.

"Look, I'm sorry," he said, taking another tack. "You are probably right. I shouldn't have been out there performing tricks with Bullet, at least not without clearing it with you first."

"No, you shouldn't have."

Eli frowned. She might be right, but she didn't have to agree so quickly.

Worse, her voice had cracked with strain. It sounded hoarse, as if she'd been yelling—or crying.

Eli cringed. He might not have meant anything by his actions, but it was vividly apparent that Mary was hurting, and equally, that he had inadvertently been the cause of it.

Mary pinched the bridge of her nose. "It wasn't all bad. You were right to bring Bullet to the party. I wish I had thought of it first. He's got to get used to big crowds and to interact with folks without getting overexcited."

On hearing his name, Bullet trotted up to Mary and rested his chin on her knee. Absently she scratched his ears.

"He did a good job keeping his focus on you, no matter what was going on around him," she added with a soft smile that made Eli's stomach do little leaps.

"Thank you," he murmured. So she *had* been watching him. Relief washed through his chest, and something else he didn't know how to classify.

"However," she continued, "I don't know what Captain James is going to think about us spilling the beans on the program just now. I'm pretty sure he wanted to be the one to make the big announcement. You know, call the press together, that kind of thing. We just took the wind out of his sails."

What she really meant was that *he* had taken the wind out of the captain's sails. Eli's breath clogged his throat, and he coughed to relieve the strangling feeling. There wasn't much press in Serendipity, but he knew exactly what Mary meant. The folks in town loved milking big news, and a new K-9 unit for the police force definitely qualified in that category. If Captain James was ticked about the news leaking early, it would likely be on Mary's head.

No wonder she was miffed at him. But she ought to know there was no way he was going to let her take the rap for something he had done. He determined right there and then to check in with Captain James first thing in the morning and let his boss know on no uncertain terms that, if there was going to be any finger-pointing or tongue-lashing going on, it was going to be at him.

"It was my idea to bring Bullet," he admitted, "but I hadn't intended to make any kind of a formal announcement about the K-9 program. Jo kind of took that information and ran with it—right to the microphone."

"She does that sometimes, doesn't she?" Mary punctuated her question with a dry chuckle and a hiccup.

Eli was relieved to hear Mary grasping the humor in the situation, especially when she was so stressed. He'd placed an enormous weight on her and the kennel. Now it was up to him to make sure she knew he would shoulder that burden.

"Don't worry about the captain," he assured her. "I promise he'll hear what really happened from me."

"You don't have to do that."

Eli reached forward and grasped the chain of the swing just above her head. "Yes, I do. And I want to."

"Well, thank you, then."

"How is your head?"

"My what?" Mary looked confused for a moment and then pressed a hand to her forehead, above her left eye. "It's better. The cool air helps."

Eli narrowed his gaze on her. Was she really ill—or had she taken off from the party because she was miffed at him?

He thought it might be the latter, and his mind scrambled for a way to reclaim the evening.

"We never got to dance together, you and I," he murmured, wrapping his fingers over the other chain of the swing and halting her rocking motion.

She was staring up at him with her beautiful green eyes so wide and sensitive his heart wanted to burst. He could read worlds into her gaze. He tried to swallow around the lump of emotion that formed in his throat, but found he couldn't.

She was so lovely with the moon and stars

as the backdrop. In that moment, all rational thought fled, and he couldn't think about a single thing he wanted more than to frame her face with his hands and unite his lips to hers—and his heart to hers.

He could see it in her gaze, as well. The hope. The yearning.

With his heart in his throat, he leaned down, intent on making their longing a reality.

Chapter Eight

Mary stood abruptly and plowed right into Eli, the top of her head connecting solidly with his chin. He didn't know whether it was her headache or the fact that she wasn't wearing her glasses, but her depth perception was off, and she'd caught him by surprise.

"Oh, dear. I'm sorry. I'm sorry," she kept repeating. He gently laid his hands on her shoulders to help her regain her equanimity, but she wrenched herself out of his grasp.

Her eyes glinted like a trapped wild animal, and she looked ready to bolt. She started to walk away. He couldn't let her do that. Not until he'd said what he needed to say.

"Mary." His voice came out low and husky.

She stopped but did not turn.

"I'm sorry if I'm the reason you missed the social."

"You're not." He couldn't see her expression,

but her voice was too tight for him to believe she was telling the full truth.

"Not sorry?" he teased, trying to lighten the heavy mood. "Because I assure you that I am, from the bottom of my heart."

She shook her head, an incoherent groan emerging from deep inside her.

"Hey, you know, I was thinking." He would keep trying. "I've never actually had the pleasure of dancing with you." It was half a statement, half an invitation.

This crazy idea popped into his head. He must have seen it in a movie, because the notion would never have come to him on his own. He'd sweep her into his arms and waltz her through the moonlight. She'd have to notice him then, right?

In reality, his execution would no doubt be none-too-pretty, especially given that there was no music out here but the occasional howl of a coyote, and he didn't even know how to waltz, anyway, so the idea very well might not be nearly as romantic as it appeared to be when he'd watched it in a movie. But now that the thought had filled his head, it refused to be set aside. He'd already come to the conclusion that Mary hadn't left the social because of a headache so much as because she'd been distressed over his actions, and he desperately wanted to make it up to her.

Mary turned, her gaze meeting his. He thought he saw the beginning of tears shimmering in her eyes, but a cloud obscured the moonlight, and he was left guessing. Her lips moved awry, giving her a particularly vulnerable expression.

Two steps and he would have his arms around her. He could fashion it as the beginning of that dance he'd quasi-offered, but in reality, he just wanted to hold her against his chest and feel her heart beating with his, sheltering her and lending her his strength until hers returned.

He took one step forward before crashing to a standstill at her next words.

"Yes. You have."

"What?" He shook his head in confusion. He had done what? He reached for her shoulders, but she shifted backward, out of his reach.

"You've danced with me before." She sniffed and gave a self-effacing chuckle. "I'm not surprised you don't remember."

Eli frowned, searching the depths of his memory for the occasion in question. Surely he'd remember it if he'd ever danced with her.

She scoffed and started walking, Bullet closely following behind her. The dog understood what Eli apparently did not—that he was in the wrong, somehow. Again. Bullet wouldn't be the one sleeping in the doghouse tonight.

Pride asserted itself in Eli's chest. He was all for manning up to his mistakes and taking responsibility for his actions, but Mary was talking plain gibberish.

And she was walking away. Even his own dog had snubbed him.

Eli huffed and burst into a jog to catch up to her. He was going to see her safely home, even if she wasn't speaking to him for who-knew-what reason.

"Hey, I'm sorry." For what, he didn't know, but it seemed like the right thing to say. He'd watched his parents' relationship through the years before his mother's passing, and had witnessed firsthand that it never hurt to apologize first and then learn why afterward. At the very least, it would buy him time to figure out what was really going on.

"No, don't," she snapped, increasing her pace.

"Don't what?"

"Don't apologize for not remembering anything. I wouldn't expect you to. You're just being nice, because that's the kind of man you are. You always have been."

They turned the corner onto her street. Her residence was only four houses down—not much time for Eli to work through this issue and come to the root of whatever was bothering Mary. He didn't want the night to end without at least knowing why she was upset.

He was certain he'd missed something major. In the back of his mind, he continued to scan for facts. He wanted to tell her that she'd missed his point. That all evening he'd been looking forward to—

That was it.

"As I recall," he drawled, loosely draping an arm around her shoulder and choosing to ignore the twinge of her muscles beneath his hand, "once upon a time, there was a girl at her first social, a pretty young thing looking a little lost and a great deal overwhelmed by it all."

"You do remember," she whispered, her wide green eyes encountering his for the slightest moment before she looked away.

"Darlin', there is no way I would forget."

And there wasn't. Not now. That long-ago encounter sizzled into his memory like a brand on livestock. The first time they'd ever danced together. He'd been no more than a kid, but even then he remembered being drawn to her.

He was amazed at how much it had taken to point him in the right direction— back to Mary, the girl he should have noticed all along.

She'd always been there, right on the out skirts of his existence, but it wasn't until he'd been forced to work with her that he'd come to see how truly remarkable she was. She outshone even the depths of his fear.

His mind and heart were so full, praising and thanking God for directing the circumstances of his life the way He had, that he didn't immediately realize Mary had walked away from him—and was, in fact, already at her door, with the key in the lock.

How could he have missed her movement, much less the cacophony of barking dogs behind her front door?

Before he could talk himself out of it, he sprang toward her porch, reaching for her key and turning it in the lock to give him time to reorient and make a plan.

Nothing. He had nothing.

He turned the doorknob and stepped aside so she could enter, but as she was passing, he took her elbow.

She glanced up at him, a pained expression on her face. Maybe that headache really was bothering her more than she cared to admit.

"Was there something else?" she asked, with a pointed look toward the spot where his hand met her arm.

"No, I…I…" he stammered. He shook his head, then thought better of it and nodded. "Yes. There is one thing."

Their gazes locked, and for a moment Eli thought of nothing beyond the beating of his own pulse. He couldn't breathe, couldn't think. Didn't want to. His only desire was to remain caught up in this moment for a lifetime. Every aspect was stamped indelibly in his heart. Her eyes. Her scent. The complex mix of emotions flooding her gaze.

"Happy Valentine's Day," he murmured, his voice little more than a whisper. Slowly, softly, he planted a lingering kiss against the smoothness of her cheek.

"Oh!" She slapped a hand over her face and cried out as if he had stung her. Before he could stop her, she rushed through the door with Bullet on her heels, slamming it shut so firmly that the sound reverberated against the quiet night air.

Eli stood frozen in time, staring mutely at the thick oak door, absorbing the painful impact of her rejection. He felt as if all the emotions he'd been experiencing had exploded, lodging shrapnel in his gut, his lungs, his throat.

And most of all, his heart.

He raised a fisted hand to knock, then realized she probably wouldn't answer no matter how hard he pounded.

With a sigh that reached the depths of his being, he stuffed his hands into the pockets of his black leather jacket and turned away to what felt like an enormously long, lonely walk back to the community center. There would be no party for him. He didn't even have his dog for company.

He wished he had his bike. Because he just wanted to ride away from it all.

Mary leaned her forehead against the door and squeezed her eyes tightly closed, but tears still managed to escape from beneath the lids. The throbbing in her head was almost unbearable, but the pain wasn't even in the same league as that of her heart. Which was, in a word, shredded.

She placed a hand to her cheek where Eli had kissed her. It still felt warm—or maybe it was the blush she knew stained her face.

Eli had the ability to take her heart and mind and emotions and juggle them around until she was so dizzy she couldn't even see straight. Then he'd toss them all high in the air where they would free-fall back to earth.

And the worst part was, he didn't even know of his effect on her.

If only he wasn't such a nice guy. She wanted to be angry with him for stringing her along this evening, as if she actually meant something to him—and she would be angry, if it wasn't Eli she was talking about.

He obviously felt obligated to her in some way, probably because they worked together. By his code of honor, no doubt it was up to the gentleman to see his ailing trainer home from the social, even at the expense of his own party plans.

Or maybe—and now that she thought of it, it seemed like the most reasonable possibility—Alexis had suggested Eli chase after her. Of course he would agree, in order to please Alexis. It made sense.

It also made Eli's actions worth less than nothing where Mary was concerned.

Oh, he was still the nice guy—he'd taken good care of her and had accompanied her all the way to her doorstep, but in the end, it was his motivation that counted the most, and that was most likely a bid to make Alexis happy.

Not that that was a bad thing, on the surface—there was nothing wrong with a man going the extra mile for the lady of his choosing, in order to please her and make her happy.

What was awful was the way his actions had inadvertently left a permanent mark on Mary. Her thoughts were full to bursting with a memory she knew she would have difficulty removing from the forefront of her mind—Eli's gentle touch. The softness of his gaze as he had wished her a happy Valentine's Day. The warmth of his breath. The musky, lingering scent of his aftershave. The sweet brush of his lips against her cheek and the deep rumble from his throat that punctuated the action.

The fact that it was a friendly kiss that meant absolutely nothing in the grand scheme of his existence.

Of course, she had no right to blame him for being a good man, especially given the way she'd scolded him. Not many men would have responded to that by insisting on seeing her home. He deserved an apology, straight from her lips. Perhaps even an explanation, were she to be so brave. In any event, she needed to return his dog to him.

Tomorrow morning, first thing, she would find him and talk to him—though finding him might prove to be problematic. Saturday was the one day a week where she didn't know how he spent his time. Monday through Friday he was with her, training Bullet, and he never missed Sunday services.

But Saturday? It was hard to say. He'd said he was a morning person, but maybe he slept in that one day a week. She knew for sure that he was a runner. Perhaps that was how he preferred to spend his weekend mornings.

No matter. Serendipity wasn't that large. She had no doubt she would find him, even if she had to comb the town from end to end and ask everyone she met for his whereabouts.

And when she found him, she would set things right. Or at least, she hoped she'd be able to do so. For the rest of the evening, she had a lot of serious praying and soul-searching to do.

The first thing Eli noticed when he stepped outside that morning was how overcast it was. Black clouds loomed overhead, and the wind picked up the moment he left the house. But bad weather wasn't going to keep him inside. In fact, it rather matched his mood at the moment.

He'd woken early and spent the first part of the morning pacing. Before long, the four walls of his apartment were closing in on him. He needed fresh air simply to breathe.

He'd briefly considered taking a long bike ride, jetting out of town and not looking back, but he was antsy and had too much energy to burn.

Instead, he put on gray sweatpants, a black hoodie and his running shoes, then headed for the park, where there was a nice greenbelt and jogging trails. Not only would he get a good run in, but his heart was always uplifted watching the oodles of children amusing themselves on the playground, not to mention extended families—grandparents, parents and children—out together, happy just spending time in each other's company.

That was what he wanted, what he'd worked for. All the years he'd kept his head down, focusing all his energy on his career—it was all for that dream in the distance. A family.

His family.

And to think he'd almost blown it by marrying Natalie. What a disaster that would have been. She wouldn't have been the least interested in settling down and raising a family. He could only thank God for looking out for him. The saying *hindsight was twenty-twenty* popped into his mind. And how true it was. What he'd once seen as the most devastating and humiliating moment of his life was actually a turning point for him, a stepping stone, a growth experience, leading him to something—some*one*—far more precious. He was sure now that he was ready to love again—in fact, he was more than halfway certain that he was already there.

Of course, that didn't solve all of his problems. He still had issues, like facing the fact that Mary had literally slammed the door on him the night before. She'd made it perfectly clear that she didn't want to speak to him.

Ouch.

Overcoming that wouldn't be easy, especially with no insight as to what made Mary tick—or in this case, what had made her *ticked*. At him. Whatever it was, it was enough for even Bullet to reject him in favor of Mary's company. But he wasn't going to give her up. He couldn't.

Eli heard his name being called and turned toward the female voice. He jogged in place to keep his heart rate up as he waited for Alexis to approach.

She waved at him, but it took her a minute to reach him in the cowboy boots she always wore. She was a Texas-born country girl through and through.

"Where are your kids?" he asked as she drew near.

"Back at the ranch. Mucking stalls under the supervision of their counselors."

Eli chuckled. "Tough love."

"The worst kind," Alexis agreed with a smile that would rival that of the Cheshire cat.

"Was there something you needed?" he asked, leading her back to the point. Wind rustled through Eli's hair, causing a lock to drop over his forehead. He threaded it back with his fingers, but it didn't really help—the wind was getting stronger.

"Big storm today, huh?" Alexis asked, noting the movement. "I haven't seen any lightning yet, but I still worry about the kids crawling all over the playground equipment. Not the safest place to be in a thunderstorm, if you ask me."

"No, it sure isn't," Eli agreed. "I guess we Texas stock are tough and resilient. We string our moments of happiness along to the last possible second."

"That was actually what I wanted to talk to you about," Alexis said.

"Oh?" Eli didn't understand the transition, if there was one. But he stopped running in place for now.

"Of course. You know—last night, you walking Mary home from the social. A happy moment for you both, I hope?"

Wow. Now that was straight and to the point. No confusion in that statement—except for the fact that he didn't have much of an answer for her, or at least not one she'd be pleased to hear.

"Not exactly." He shrugged, but it was a jerky movement and not the casual action he was shooting toward.

Alexis frowned and crossed her arms against the wind. "Why? What happened?"

"Well, apart from Mary slamming the door in my face, I'd have to say it was more about what *didn't* happen."

"She didn't!" Alexis clapped a hand over her

mouth, first in shock, and then to cover up her laughter. As if he couldn't hear her giggling from behind her palm. He quirked a grin, even if he personally didn't believe there was anything to smile about.

She shook her head and swatted his shoulder. "You must have done something horrible to her. Mary would never do anything like that without provocation—especially to you."

"Well, she did," Eli grumbled. "And why would you say *especially* to me?"

"If you can't figure that out, Elijah Bishop, then you have a good deal less brain matter than I gave you credit for."

"Why, thank you," he replied wryly, but hope stirred in his chest. Was he totally misreading her, or was she implying that Mary might have tender feelings for him after all? "The truth of the matter is that I'm at a complete loss. I'm the first to admit I'm no expert when it comes to reading women. But Mary, she's just…all over the place emotionally. I know it's not easy for her, being that I was once engaged to Natalie. But there are moments when we really connect, and then the next thing I know—well, she's slamming doors in my face, either literally or figuratively."

"She's scared."

"Of what? Me?"

"Not you, exactly, but I think she's frightened of herself and her feelings for you. She doesn't want to get hurt. And she doesn't want to lose you as a friend, if things don't work out between you."

"But she won't lose me as a friend," Eli protested. "If I have my way, we'll have much more. We'll grow closer and mean that much more to each other."

"And that is the scariest thing of all, because from those heights, it's a long way to fall."

"I think I get it," Eli said, compassion and compulsion simultaneously welling in his chest. He was a man of action, not so much a purveyor of feelings. He wanted to fix the problem. "I've got to come right out and set her straight about my own position. After Natalie, she's bound to have questions and concerns. I can put her mind at ease where my feelings for her are concerned. I simply need to be candid."

"That's what I've been saying all along!" She punched his shoulder playfully. "Go get her, cowboy."

"I will," he said, determining right then and there not to waste any more time. He would find Mary and tell her the truth. About everything. She didn't know about his phobia, and she didn't know about his affection for her.

No. More than affection.

He hadn't said the words aloud—but he was ready. And he wanted to say them directly to Mary.

At the first sight of Eli and Alexis together, Mary slipped behind the biggest oak tree she could find. Her pulse was racing and dread filled her stomach.

And then it started to rain.

Of all the scenarios she'd envisioned since last night's escapades, finding Eli and Alexis engrossed in a conversation out in public together was not among them. From the looks of things, they were pretty close, what with Alexis playfully flirting and Eli responding, beaming like an incandescent lightbulb.

Anyone with eyes could see how perfect Eli and Alexis were together. Gorgeous, blonde Alexis with Mr. Tall, Dark and Handsome himself.

"Bullet. Sebastian. *Volg*," she whispered harshly when the dogs spotted Eli and bolted forward in anticipation.

Mary wished she'd left the dogs at home, but Bullet was her excuse for hunting Eli down on his only day off. Now she was beginning to regret that decision. The dogs were acting particularly squirrely, perhaps because of the weather. If they didn't calm down, she was bound to get all kinds of attention, and attention was the last thing she needed right now.

After what felt like an excruciatingly long time, but was probably no more than about a minute, Alexis took off. Eli stayed where he was, watching the children on the playground, his hands tucked into the single front pocket of his black hoodie.

Mary sighed and stayed plastered to the trunk of the oak, not caring that the rough bark was cutting into her palms. The superficial pain gave her something else to think about, something other than the blade slicing her insides apart.

Go, Eli. Just go.

If she could will it to be so, Eli would finish whatever he was doing and take up his run again, returning to the jogging path and letting Mary off the hook.

That it was still sprinkling didn't really register. Not in the mood she was in. She barely even noticed that the air had the funny electrical feeling that usually accompanied a lightning storm, and the sky glowed twilight, though it was morning.

She *did* notice when the sky suddenly lit up like a room full of fluorescent lights, and not even a second later, the cracking boom of thunder made the ground shake underneath her feet.

The children on the playground started screaming and scattering as parents scrambled to find their kids in the pandemonium that ensued.

It was utter chaos. Mary could barely see through the torrential downpour that quickly began, and what the rain was lacking, the wind provided, making sheets out of the rainwater and blowing eaves from the houses surrounding the park.

Mary knew what kind of danger they were facing. This storm had come out of nowhere. It wouldn't be the first time they'd faced tornadoes during the winter months. As few and far between as they were, they weren't completely unheard of. And they were always devastating.

Forgetting her own troubles for the moment, she darted out from behind the giant oak and strove to round up a group of older children who had been hanging around the park unsupervised, and who were now heading toward the open street.

The storm was quickly building momentum. Lightning flashed, and then flashed again. Thunder echoed one roll after another. The wind howled eerily. Trees swayed precariously, their branches waving in distress.

"Kids," she called, loud enough for them to

be able to hear her over the wind. "Come this way. Hurry."

To her relief, they heeded her call, turning as a group and gathering around her. Left on their own, they'd scatter to their own residences. Several of the kids lived a few blocks from the park. Some even farther. Much better they seek shelter in the nearby chapel.

"I checked my cell," said a deep voice from behind her. She didn't have to turn to know it was Eli. Bullet had already switched allegiance and was now trailing Eli, while Sebastian continued to stand at her side.

"Storm warning?" she guessed. She had to admit all the noise and sound had her a little worried.

"More than that," he replied grimly, pressing his lips in a tight line. "As of this morning, meteorologists were already predicting large hail and damaging winds, but now they are saying there's the possibility of early tornadoes. It's a supercell—hitting Oklahoma, as well. The wind is expected to reach up to ninety miles per hour. We're looking at something pretty major here."

Mary's mind was spinning. No wonder the dogs were jumpy. It was worse than she'd originally imagined. "Then there's the possibility of major damage."

Eli nodded and slicked his wet hair back with his palm.

"Head for the church," she instructed the kids. The chapel was the closer of the two designated storm shelters in Serendipity, the other being the community center across town. "Go straight there. No dillydallying. Do you understand? And phone your parents when you get there, so they know you're safe."

Mary and Eli spent the next half hour rounding up frightened residents and making sure they knew to take refuge in the church. She prayed that those who hadn't claimed safety within one of the designated shelters were at least batting down the hatches in their homes and seeking safe areas to wait out the storm. She was determined to do what she could to help those who needed it.

The rain was bad, the wind was worse, but when it all stopped suddenly, the real terror began.

"Do you see it?" Eli called, his eyes to the sky.

Mary didn't have to ask what *it* was.

A tornado.

"No," she shouted back, "but I can feel it."

"Me, too. Shall we head for the church?"

Mary nodded. Eli reached for her hand and they ran full tilt toward the chapel, increasing their pace even more when the town's tornado sirens started shrilling. As much as she wanted to make sure everyone else in town was safe, it was imperative at this point that they look after themselves and the dogs that ran at their heels. They'd held out as long as they possibly could, and there would be much to do yet today. As it was now, the church would be crowded with frightened townfolk. Pastor Shawn would need all the help he could get to keep everyone calm and collected once they started hearing the tornado sirens.

The pause in the storm was followed by another downpour, sheets of rain that drenched them both instantly. She could hardly see going forward and relied heavily on Eli's guidance. Still, she was caught off guard when he suddenly yanked her back and sheltered her in his arms. His shoulders blocked the brunt of the sudden explosion and a shower of electrical sparks that rained over them as a tree fell into a power line.

"Are you okay?" he asked, brushing her hair back from her face so he could see her eyes. "Did the sparks get you?"

"That was way too close for comfort," Mary answered, gritting her teeth against the terrified sob that was fighting for release from her throat. "But I'm okay." She cringed and ducked when she heard the pop-pop of windows breaking in the distance.

He met her gaze with a determined set to his jaw. "Come on. We can do this. Not too much farther to the chapel now."

As Eli ran, he kept his arm around Mary's waist, sometimes half dragging her when she slipped or slowed. She focused on his warmth, his strength and his determination to get them both to the safety of the church.

At last she could make out the steeple and the welcoming red doors. They slipped inside, and Mary gasped, glad to be out of the worst of the weather. She knew the rampant surge of emergencies due to the storm's fury were only beginning for her and for the town. The worst was yet to come.

The lights flickered in the narthex as they headed toward an interior, windowless room where they found many townspeople hovering around an NOAA weather radio broadcasting an emergency alert. The blaring beep echoed throughout the otherwise silent room as everyone stayed attuned to hear the worst—that tornadoes had been sighted in their area and were threatening their beloved town.

"What do you say we make these people more comfortable?" Eli suggested, reaching for a thick pile of blankets and nodding for her to start spreading them across the floor. When that was finished, he reached for a case of bottled water while she opened up a large container of kids' fruit snacks. They circled the room, handing out the bounty and reassuring them that all would be well.

No one had officially put the two of them in charge. Mary understood why the community instinctively looked to Eli for guidance— he was a man with a badge, usually in uniform, a deputy sheriff.

But for some unexplainable reason, folks were actively seeking her out, listening for her counsel. How could they possibly expect her to blunder into a leadership position? Was it because she'd come through the door with Eli and was clearly working in tandem with him? Or was it because she had Sebastian at her heel, just as Eli had Bullet for company?

She didn't have long to ponder those questions, for more people started streaming into the church, soaking wet and brimming with terrifying stories of what was happening outside. The noise level heightened along with the tension. A few folks had injuries, mostly minor, thankfully—straining a muscle or spraining an ankle in their hurry to get to the shelter of the church. Mary was fairly sure one young boy had a broken arm. The poor kid had been up in a tree when the big wind hit and had fallen several feet to the ground in his haste to climb back down again. There were also a good number of bumps and bruises from flying debris, and a few lacerations from encounters with broken windows.

Old Frank was complaining—loudly—that he couldn't find his wife. Mary didn't see Jo, either, but she didn't see any reason to panic yet. For all they knew, Jo was holed up at the community center or back at her house. At any rate, she had a good head on her shoulders and wouldn't be taking any unnecessary risks. Of that, Mary was certain.

"Easy there, Frank," she consoled firmly, knowing he wouldn't want a soft approach. "Jo is fine. You know her. Well able to take care of herself in any given situation. She's one tough woman."

Frank snorted. "You got that right. Stubborn as all get-out, too."

"There, so you see? No worries. We'll catch up with her soon, I'm sure."

She patted Frank's shoulder and then worked her way through the crowd, heading toward Eli, who had one hand clamped over his ear to make it easier to hear whomever he was speaking to on his cell phone. At a head taller than most other folks, he was easy to see, but not so easy to reach in the cramped quarters of the church safe room. By the time she got to his side, he'd ended his phone call.

"Where are Zach and Ben?" she asked, naming the two paramedics who volunteered at the tricounty fire station. "Or Delia?" Delia was Zach's wife and the town doctor.

"I just got off the phone with Zach," he said, sliding his cell back into the single pocket of his black hoodie.

"They were on duty at the firehouse?" she asked. The volunteer fire station was located near the community center, as was the police department, so most of those serving in an official capacity for the town were probably holed up at the other authorized shelter location.

"He and Ben are both at the community center. Wouldn't you know they were playing basketball together at the center when the storm warning came through. Zach and Delia are going to brave the storm and head this direction, since it appears we have more wounded than they do, but it will be a while before they get here."

"So they don't have many wounded—yet."

Eli nodded solemnly. "That's right."

Maybe it was the fact that she'd lived her whole life in Serendipity and knew what kinds of battles they fought with the weather, or maybe it was the unusually warm, electrical feeling in the air, but she had a gut feeling the storm wasn't over with.

There was a burst of energy that brightened the fluorescent lights over their heads, and then the room pitched into darkness. Mary couldn't see a thing, not even Eli, who was standing right next to her. Maybe it was the lack of one physical sense that made another so intense, because it was so much more than simply the gift of touch when Eli threaded his fingers through hers. She felt it with every nerve ending, every spot where their hands made contact. He communicated protection and strength without words and brought the definition of *hero* to a whole new level.

Pastor Shawn flipped the switch on a bright LED lantern, and the moment of panic was over. Eli dropped her hand when he was given a flashlight for himself, and then he helped the pastor pass out the remaining lights, including one for Mary.

The silence passed, and some of those around her struck up conversations—not about the storm or the wind or the tornado but about the success of the Sweetheart Social, and how they were looking forward to the next community event. There was even some light laughter in parts of the room.

It seemed counterintuitive, but Mary could relate. These folks didn't want to think of the storm's devastation or the possibility that there was more to come. Yes, they'd deal with whatever damage was done, and bravely, at that, but for now, they were together, and they were safe, and that was all that mattered. The people.

"How are you with sprains?" Eli asked, coming up behind her and laying a soothing hand on her shoulder.

"I'm an expert, remember?" she said, trying to lighten the mood a little, if only because she felt her own alarm so keenly. She smiled up at him, taking a tip from the folks here at the shelter. "I can't believe you forgot having to carry me a mile across the Texas plain."

"I didn't forget," he murmured from deep in his throat. One side of his lips quirked upward. "And I guess that does make you an expert. Samantha twisted her ankle on the way over here from her store. I'm sure she would appreciate having you wrap it for her—since, obviously, you know what you're doing. Pastor Shawn has a bandage."

"What about you? Where will you be?" She felt the oddest moment of panic jolt through her chest and into her head when she considered him going somewhere without her—especially out in that storm.

He pulled up the hood of his sweatshirt, a determined expression on his face. "I'm going out to make sure there aren't any stragglers left on Main Street—just in case anyone needs help getting to the shelter. I think the tornado might have vectored off, but there is still a heavy wind. I expect there's probably a great deal of damage, and I don't want anyone out walking in it when they could be safe inside the shelter."

She laid a hand on his forearm. "Let me come with you. We both have SAR dogs, remember? Bullet and Sebastian are both trained to find humans under exigent circumstances. They can do what we can't. I'm sure Will can see to Samantha's injury."

Eli blanched. He glanced down at Bullet and ran a hand across his jaw. "I've got to be honest here. I wasn't thinking about working with the dog. I'm afraid I'll be more of a hindrance than a help out there, if we're trying to do this with the dogs. If the dogs are the best choice for finding people then maybe I'd be of more use here, organizing the troops, so to speak, than in doing any real search and rescue."

He started to turn away, but Mary tightened her grip on his elbow.

"Don't you dare walk away from me, Elijah Bishop," she demanded in a voice worthy of a police captain.

Eli's gaze widened in surprise, but he stayed where he was, his mouth in a firm, straight and very stubborn line.

"You aren't giving yourself enough credit," she continued. "Have you any idea how far you've come in the past month?"

He scowled and shook his head. "Not far enough."

"You think? Well, there you're wrong, and you're going to listen to the truth right now. No, we haven't quite completed your search-and-rescue training, since I was saving the best for last. But you have worked with Bullet on all types of terrain and in any number of critical situations. This isn't that much different.

"Bullet trusts you. Believe me when I say you can do more good out there with me, performing search-and-rescue tactics with Bullet that only you can do, than in standing around here passing out water bottles, straightening blankets and reassuring folks that all is well. Although, of course, you're good at that, too."

She winked at him and then blushed at her own audacity. The adrenaline of the moment must be getting to her. She couldn't believe she'd just talked to Eli that way. Even more baffling was the fact that he appeared to be carefully considering her words.

"What do you want me to do?"

He was letting her take the lead, looking to her for direction. The notion was so foreign to her that she wanted to duck and run for cover. She knew SAR tactics, but this was an unusual situation. She didn't know how to take command. The dressing-down she'd given him had shifted the situation just a bit too far in an uncomfortable direction.

Mary had been a follower all her life. She didn't question authority—and most of the time, saw no reason to. She never made waves. She stayed in the shadow of her friends and lived her life on the outside fringes.

Until now.

She closed her eyes for a moment and searched deep within herself, seeking the capacity for leadership that she hadn't even known she possessed.

Once again the nerve endings in her fingers went wild when Eli covered her hand with his. Her eyes shot open to find him gazing at her with an intensity that surprised her.

"Let's pray before we head out," he suggested.

Mary was so lost in the fervor of his blue eyes that she could do no more than nod. Her heart welled up with so much emotion she thought she might burst. Now was not the time to acknowledge her love for Eli, much less analyze it, and yet it was the perfect time, for this was Eli at his strongest. He bent his head, until his forehead touched hers, and whispered prayers for protection and guidance—not only for themselves, but for anyone they should meet along the way.

"Where to?" he asked after they'd agreed in prayer with a soft *amen*.

"I think we should head out to Main Street, as you suggested, and see what kind of damage we're looking at. First stop, Cup O' Jo's Café. Frank's worried that he can't find Jo—more even than he's letting on. I'd like to put his mind at ease."

Eli nodded in agreement, and held the door for her and Sebastian to pass through. It was a gentlemanly gesture, but also a necessary one, as the wind hadn't let up much, and the door might have broken free of its hinges, were it not for Eli's sheer strength.

Hand in hand with their dogs at their sides, Mary and Eli crossed the street to where the café was located. Mary was happy to see it was all in one piece, although the old clapboard welcome sign that stretched across the top of the doorway was dangling precariously from one hook. Eli reached up and forced the sign off the hook. She knew what he was thinking. It wouldn't take much to repair the damage, and that way no one could get hurt if the sign suddenly gave way.

Emerson's Hardware, located next door to the café, hadn't been so fortunate. The front window was blown out, either from the wind or from flying debris, and there was shattered glass all along the sidewalk. In a large city, such a sight would have been prime diggings for looting and stealing, but Mary knew that, here in Serendipity, the hardware store's biggest concern and challenge would be replacing the window and dealing with any other storm-related damage. Theft probably wouldn't be much of an issue.

She glanced up and down Main Street, but so far, thankfully, they hadn't seen any stragglers.

"Should we check inside the buildings?" Eli asked. "Just in case anyone is trapped inside?"

"Good idea," she agreed. "You take Jo's café and I'll check Emerson's. Remember to keep yourself on safe ground and let Bullet do the exploring. He's used to searching through rough debris."

She was confident in the dogs' tracking abilities, but there was still a moment when her heart caught in her throat, and she doubted all the work she'd done. Today's events were going to make or break her. In terms of her future with Rapport Kennels, this was where the rubber met the road.

Chapter Nine

Eli kept his eye on Mary as she and Sebastian carefully navigated through the front door of Emerson's, fighting the wind every step of the way. He thought it might have been less of a hassle for her simply to crawl through the barren window, but then he realized there were sharp fragments of shattered glass on the ground and, while Mary was fairly protected in her tennis shoes, Sebastian's paws were exposed.

It was a good reminder for him—he was no longer an individual policeman, but working as a unit. It was up to him to consider not only what was best for himself but also his partner—Bullet.

"Okay, boy," he said to the soaking-wet dog staring at him, waiting for a command. "It's time for us to prove our worth to the community—and especially to Mary. You know what I'm saying, don't you, boy?"

Bullet barked.

Eli chuckled. "No more kiddie tricks for us. This is the real thing."

Bullet seemed to understand, because Eli noted the immediate change in his demeanor. The dog was on full alert, his ears pricked forward and his muscles tensed—and that was before Eli had even issued a vocal command or gestured for him to scan.

He shone his flashlight through the dining area. The inside of the café looked untouched by the weather, other than the half-eaten plates of food on several of the tables, where patrons had obviously left in a hurry in the middle of their meals. Bullet immediately went to work examining the tables and underneath the chairs. Eli was proud of the dog for not being distracted by the scent of the food.

Mary had done an excellent job training Bullet. She deserved all the best God could bless her with—including contracts for K-9 units from all the surrounding neighborhood police departments.

Eli realized he could help her with that. He had contacts, and he could use them. He was thrilled to think there was something he could do to bless Mary as she had blessed him—he could introduce her to the right people, the decision makers. Maybe he could even present Bullet as a shining example of her work.

He'd always believed God would use his strengths to minister to others. The realization that the Lord could use his weaknesses and vulnerabilities was like an emotional knock to the head. Using his work with a dog to help people? He was humbled and amazed.

To think of the way he'd fought this life change when it had first been presented to him. Maybe not as much on the outside—he wasn't about to turn down the promotion or leave himself open for more merciless teasing by his friends on the force—but he'd certainly battled it inwardly. Every step forward had been excruciating, and he'd given Mary a hard time in the process, when all she had been trying to do was help him.

Apparently he was one of those men—the most stubborn kind, he suspected—who had to be strong-armed into change and into making the right decisions. He was guilty of taking too much at face value and not looking deeper to find true worth.

Like Mary. Now there was true gold.

Eli paused in his thoughts as Bullet neared the window that separated the dining area from the kitchen. Even before the dog marked a strong hit by sitting, Eli was aware of the change in Bullet's demeanor. Even from a distance and with nothing but a flashlight to see with, he could read the dog's progress—*feel* it. It was the most remarkable sensation.

Eli hadn't yet moved from beyond the threshold of the restaurant, but after Bullet presented a clear hit, sitting before the window with his focus not wavering, Eli knew it was time to move.

"What have you got, boy?" he murmured, feeling suddenly unsure of himself. Was he supposed to throw the tennis ball for Bullet now, or wait until he knew for sure that the dog had actually found something?

"Hello?" he called, loud enough to be heard over the storm. His voice echoed in the vacant room. "Is anyone here?"

"Is it over?" Jo's voice came from somewhere in the vicinity of the kitchen. "I still hear a lot of wind. The tornado is gone, though, right?"

Eli tossed the ball for Bullet. "Good boy! Good boy!"

"I beg your pardon. Who are you calling *boy?*"

He chuckled. If Jo was joking around, she couldn't be injured too badly.

He went around the service island and entered the kitchen. One look at Jo sprawled in a corner with her shoulder up against a crooked cabinet and her hip at an awkward angle caused him to change his opinion.

What was he supposed to do now? All the first-aid training he'd received at the police academy deserted him in a rush.

Blank. Absolute, total blank.

What use was he? He wished that he and Mary had been able to finish the search-and-rescue part of their K-9 training. He felt certain she would know what to do. They hadn't gotten as far as tracking people, much less what to do when he found one. And an injured woman, at that.

If he was on duty, he could at least call it in and potentially get some medical backup. As it was, he didn't have his radio on him, and he wouldn't know who to call if he did. Serendipity was such a small town that most things, even emergencies, were handled in a rather casual fashion. The medics and the town doctor already had their hands full at the shelters.

He crouched before Jo and laid a comforting hand on her shoulder. Bullet nosed his way under her arm and licked her cheek.

She chuckled. A good sign, right?

"Are you in pain? What exactly happened here? Your hubby is throwing fits back at the chapel because he couldn't find you."

"Old goat," she muttered.

"True," Eli agreed with a dry chuckle. "But he sure does love you."

Jo laughed and then grimaced.

So she *was* in pain. Eli pressed his lips, trying to recall the first-aid lessons he'd had. He hadn't had much cause to use them up until now.

"Eli?" Mary called from the dining room. "Are you in the back? I checked out Emerson's, and other than the fact that they've got a big mess to clean up, what with all the glass and everything, there's nothing to—"

Her sentence came to an abrupt end as she turned the corner into the kitchen and saw Jo sprawled on the floor.

"Oh, my. Jo. What happened?" Mary's mouth moved but no further words surfaced. Eli thought she might be praying. Why hadn't he thought of that, at least?

"Don't panic, dear. My life is safe in Eli's capable hands. A regular knight in shining armor, this one."

Eli snorted and shook his head. As if he had been any use to Jo at all. Hindrance, more like.

"He and this handsome fur ball here came to my rescue. I don't have a thing to worry about." She scratched Bullet's ear, and he leaned into her, clearly enjoying the attention.

Mary knelt and visually assessed Jo's situation. "Can you tell me what happened?" she asked, clearly to keep Jo talking while she checked for injuries. "Does anything hurt? How's your hip?"

"If my hip is out, it's my own fault."

"How do you figure?" Eli asked.

Jo reached out to him and gingerly shifted her weight his direction, into a full sitting position. "Help me stand up, honey, and I'll give you the rundown. Quite humiliating, being caught in this position."

"Don't be ridiculous," Mary assured her. "There's nothing to be embarrassed about. Not to Eli and me."

He couldn't have said it better. Mary had such a tender heart, and it showed in every word and gesture. How could he not fall for a woman like that?

With Eli at one elbow and Mary at the other, Jo leveraged herself to her feet. She tested her hip and pronounced it good.

"When the wind started a-blowin' like there was no tomorrow, I knew something wacky was up. I could feel it in these old bones—and believe you me, they never lie. Complain like crazy, most of the time, but they're never wrong about the weather."

She sighed and leaned against the counter. No matter how she protested to the contrary, she still looked like she'd been through the wringer.

Eli was well aware of how stubborn she was, so he unobtrusively hovered close to her side, ready to catch her if her hip gave out.

"I shooed all them folks in the dining room out to the shelter at the chapel, whether they were done eatin' or not. I've lived long enough to know you don't mess around with a Texas storm. Might be nothing, or it might become a supercell in a matter of minutes and knock you into next Friday. Better safe than sorry, I always say."

"What about you?" Eli asked, quirking his lips to rein in a chuckle. Count on Jo to have one piece of advice for the rest of the world while she completely ignored that very same wisdom herself. "You're not taking your own advice, nowadays?"

"Don't you be mouthin' off to me, young man," Jo said, swatting his shoulder. That Eli wasn't remotely close to a young man only made the moment more comical. "I had eggs on my griddle and rolls in the oven. I couldn't very well leave without shutting everything down, storm or no storm. The weather was enough of a threat without me goin' and burnin' my own place to the ground."

"And then you got trapped when the worst of the storm hit?" Mary asked.

"In a way. I guess I may have panicked there

for a moment." She shook her head so hard her mop of red hair bounced in rhythm.

Jo Spencer? Panicking? Now that *was* unbelievable.

"The tornado didn't hit the town, did it?"

Eli shook his head. "Not so far as we know. It was heading straight for us at one point, but we believe it vectored off at the last moment."

"Well, thanks be to God for that," Jo exclaimed, waving her hands in the air.

"Amen," Mary agreed.

"There was a lot of wind damage, though," Eli added. "It'll take a while for the town to pick up the pieces."

"Literally and figuratively," said Mary.

"I'll tell you, I was praying up my own storm right here in that little corner of my kitchen," Jo admitted.

"Why didn't you head for the shelter yourself, after you'd turned off your oven and all?" Eli asked.

"I was going that direction, mind you, but then the tornado siren went off. I heard quite a frightening pop—it sounded like an explosion—and all I could think of to do was duck, which I did."

"Good thinking," Eli said. "That pop you heard was the front window of Emerson's bursting out. Shattered the glass clear through."

"Oh, dear. Poor Edward. No one was hurt, I gather?"

"As far as we know, no one was in the store when it happened," Mary assured her.

"Anyway, you did the right thing," said Eli.

"My poor hip doesn't think so. I dropped myself down into that corner, and then I couldn't get back up again. How humiliating is that? If you two hadn't come along, I would've been here till the cows came home."

"Or Frank came searching," Mary teased.

"Old goat," Jo said, as if in agreement to Mary's statement.

"Why don't we get you over to the chapel so one of the medics can check out that hip of yours and make sure you haven't injured it in some way. I'm sure Frank will be happy to see that you're okay."

"He's going to be grumpy about it, is what he'll be. All over me about not takin' care of myself and puttin' myself first before everything else. For the life of me, I don't know what I see in that man."

Eli and Mary both laughed. It was true that Frank and Jo were as different as two people could be—Jo with a personality that radiated sunshine and Frank as crotchety as the dark of the moon—yet somehow God had fit them together perfectly. They loved each other to distraction despite their differences—or maybe because of them.

Jo insisted on walking across the street without assistance, though both Eli and Mary stayed close enough to assist her should the need arise. Even their dogs were hovering, their combined focus intent on the old woman.

Eli met Mary's gaze and his heart warmed at her smile. It was nice to be needed and to make a real difference. He would never look at his career the same way again. After all, he'd found Jo with Bullet's assistance.

K-9 to the rescue.

"I see Stephanie Spencer coming up the road," Mary informed Eli and Jo. "I should go help her—she's at least seven months pregnant, and the wind is still acting up."

"Go get her, dear," Jo encouraged. "I'm doing just fine with Eli here to help me."

Eli nodded. "I'll catch up with you after I get Jo settled in."

Mary started down the middle of Main Street, not bothering with the clapboard sidewalks. She offered Stephanie a friendly wave to let her know she was coming, but as she neared the woman, she could see something was off. Stephanie was in clear distress. Mascara-laced tears streaked black trails down her face. Her eyes were wide and glassy, and she was cradling her stomach as if all that was keeping her going was the instinct to protect the infant within.

"Hey, Stephanie."

The woman looked right through her, and Mary's breath caught. This was bad. Really bad.

"Honey, I need you to tell me what's wrong," Mary instructed, expecting to hear something about Stephanie's fear of false labor or of stress contractions. Instead, Stephanie burst into fresh tears and started spouting unrelated words.

"The preschool. Light pole. Kids. Counted. Lost," she stammered between short, staccato breaths.

"Slow down, hon," Mary said. The woman was close to hyperventilating. What if she passed out before Mary understood what she was trying to tell her? "Something happened at the preschool?"

Stephanie had been the one to open the town's official preschool, and she served as both director and teacher there now.

Stephanie nodded miserably and took a ragged breath. "Sirens. Roof. Got the kids out. Counted. Oh. Heavenly Father. What have I done?" She slumped forward into Mary's arms.

"Lord, help us both," Mary prayed fervently. "What happened when you counted the children, Stephanie?" She cradled the woman's head and forced her to make eye contact. "You have to tell me."

"Missing." Stephanie groaned and tried once again to slump into semiconsciousness. It was clear the woman was in medical shock.

"Stephanie," Mary said again, demanding her attention. She needed to get the woman to the shelter and wrapped in a blanket, but not until she knew what was going on. "Who? Who is missing?"

Stephanie wailed, a frightening stream of emotion filtering from deep within her. "Aaron Hawkins. I thought I got them all out. I tried. I don't know. I—"

She stopped speaking and doubled over as a contraction overwhelmed her, her expression turning from sorrow to agony. Her jaw tightened, and her eyes once again took on a glassy, distant quality. She drew into herself, disappearing somewhere else in the midst of the pain.

Mary was on the verge of panic. It was almost too much for her to bear, especially on her own. A missing preschooler and a woman in premature labor. What was she supposed to do with all this? Her heart hammered and her mind raced.

She shook Stephanie's shoulders, knowing

she had to bring her back to some sense of reality, no matter how painful it was for her.

"Stephanie? Do you think you might be in labor?"

She hiccupped, then inhaled through her teeth as the contraction subsided.

"I don't know. Maybe."

"When did the contractions start, and how far apart are they? Are they regular or intermittent?"

Stephanie shook her head against the onslaught of questions.

"I don't know," she said again. "Took the kids out. Pain started. Kept coming." She slurred the words so that Mary could barely understand what she was saying.

"Where are the kids now?"

"Center. Shelter."

"Did you take them there?"

Stephanie shook her head, but offered no explanation as to what she was doing here, alone, on the opposite end of town.

This was a nightmare.

Suddenly Stephanie grasped Mary's arm so hard her fingernails bit into her skin, but Mary didn't flinch.

"This can't be labor, right?" She was begging for assurance that Mary could not give.

"I don't know. It might be. But let's not panic. How far along are you?"

"Thirty-six weeks."

"It could be Braxton Hicks. Just try to breathe through your contractions until we can get you looked at." Mary supported Stephanie around the waist and turned her directly toward the chapel. "Let's get you to the shelter. It's not far now."

"Aaron," she whimpered.

"I know, hon, but you need to see Delia."

Mary glanced backward, down the empty street. At the chapel there were many others who could do as much for Stephanie as she could, and there was a little boy missing. There was no easy answer, no solution where everybody won.

"Do you think you can make it the rest of the way to the chapel? There will be someone to meet you and take you to Delia." She took Stephanie by the shoulders and looked her right in the eyes, trying to ascertain if she could follow the simple direction.

Stephanie made a sound that passed for an affirmation.

"I promise you I'm going to find Aaron, okay? You concentrate on that little baby of yours. I'll make sure you're the first person to know that Aaron is safe."

If Aaron was safe. Please, God.

Mary was relieved to see the determined spark in Stephanie's gaze. It wasn't far for her to walk to reach the chapel. She would make it. She had to.

Mary, on the other hand, was facing her very own nightmare-come-to-life. She prayed fervently for guidance. She didn't even know where to start, but she was thankful for her search-and-rescue training and the dog at her side. Sebastian's presence reassured her. He didn't get anxious. He wanted to get the job done.

"Come on, boy," she said to her Lab. "Let's go find Aaron."

From what she could piece together from Stephanie's garbled statements, something had fallen on the roof of the preschool, and she had evacuated the children. At some point she'd stopped to count them and had realized one of them was missing—Aaron Hawkins.

She prayed Stephanie was wrong about Aaron, and the boy was safe in the shelter with the others. She had no idea why Stephanie had been out wandering the street, except that she was in shock from the accident and from the pain of her labor.

She decided a visit to the community center was in order, to get some answers there and to make sure the other children were safe. But her fear for Aaron continued to nag her, so she made a small detour to stop by and determine what had really happened to the preschool.

What she saw shocked her. The building couldn't have been more than a couple of years old, an infant dwelling compared to the nineteenth-century clapboard buildings that lined Main Street. But Stephanie was right about the damage. An electrical pole had been torn from its roots and then had fallen dead-center on the preschool's left wing, breaking out windows and caving in the roof on that side.

She was grateful Stephanie had managed to get as many children out as she had. But Aaron...

"Sebastian!" she called in a moment of panic when the dog darted into a hole made from brick and crumpled drywall. She hadn't given him any kind of command, but she knew what he was doing.

His job.

Now she needed to pull herself together and do hers.

Chapter Ten

Mary wished she wasn't alone, but she wasn't going to leave when Sebastian may have found a hit on Aaron. Digging around in the debris with the chance of a live electrical current was an enormous risk, but one she was prepared to take, if it meant saving the little boy. Sebastian had gone in on instinct, and Mary trusted her dog.

She fished her cell out of her pocket and punched in Eli's number. He'd want to be here for this, to experience search and rescue at its best. Moreover, she needed backup, which he could give her. And he could alert the medics, just in case Aaron was hurt.

She glanced at her phone, wondering why the call wasn't going through.

No signal. Not a single bar. Why was this happening? She'd never had a problem with cell reception within Serendipity town limits before.

Not now, Lord. Please.

She tapped her phone twice and then shoved it back into her pocket with a frustrated groan.

She was completely on her own. And she had a decision to make.

Did she go forward, or should she call Sebastian back?

Forward.

This was what all her training was about. Her very life's work came down to this.

One lost child.

She gritted her teeth, and with every ounce of determination she carried coursing through her veins, she moved toward the front door. It was still standing, and she didn't hesitate to enter through it, nimbly stepping through the debris, intent on finding Sebastian—and hopefully, Aaron.

"Where are you, boy?" she called, holding her flashlight at shoulder level and making a sweeping pass over the devastated area. Scattered wooden blocks, puzzles and bits of colorful stuffed animals were wedged between broken two-by-fours and shattered drywall. The back wall still stood, covered with a whiteboard and posters with the alphabet letters on them. It was a stark contrast to the destruction around it and an eerie sight.

"Sebastian?" she called again.

This time she heard him bark, followed by a hollow whine, almost as if he was trying to speak her language. Even without seeing him, she knew he'd made a hit. And the dark knot in the pit of her stomach told her it was Aaron.

She shone her light in the direction of the sound, one room over—or what would have been one room had the building still been standing. She pulled her scarf over her mouth and nose to block the dust raised from the wind sifting through the broken drywall.

She pushed aside debris with her hands, shoulders and feet, no longer caring about the threat of a live wire.

"Aaron?" she called, loud enough to be heard but gentle enough not to scare the child. If he was conscious, he was probably scared out of his wits.

Sebastian whined again. She could see him now, sitting in a full, strong hit stance, but scratching at the floor in front of him and nosing a board stretched diagonally from what was left of one wall to the floor. The roof, such as it was, was sagging, with little support from the beams. Soon it would collapse completely. If Aaron was stuck in that corner, he was in grave danger.

She had to get him out *now*.

"What've you got, boy?" She climbed over a

pile of broken tables to reach her dog. Quickly she examined the diagonal board that was blocking the corner, testing it for movement, but it didn't budge.

Then she heard a whimper.

It was the smallest sound, there for a second, and then it was gone, but it took away any doubts Mary might have had.

Little Aaron was buried somewhere underneath the rubble.

She couldn't move the diagonal plank, so rather than take up more time trying, she gingerly moved piece by agonizing piece of debris from the triangle underneath it. Her palms were soon bleeding from splinters and sharp edges, but she didn't care.

Finally she'd made a hole large enough for her to crawl into. She immediately saw Aaron slumped up against the wall, his body limp. The boy was whimpering but unconscious. Mary worried that he'd been hit in the head by flying wreckage.

She checked for external injuries and found none. She knew general medical protocol was against moving an unconscious person. An unseen neck wound might leave him permanently paralyzed.

But what was the alternative?

She glanced up at the holes in the roof. Who

knew how long those beams would hold? There was no way she was going to leave Aaron here alone while she went to get help, not with the whole building ready to collapse on top of him. And staying with him in this position wouldn't protect him, either.

Mary stared down at Aaron and blew out a cleansing breath to steady herself for what she knew must be done.

Please, Lord, let this be the right thing.

With infinite care, she curled the young child in her arms, pulling him close to her heart. He was bigger and heavier than she'd expected, but with the amount of adrenaline shooting through her, she knew they could make it.

She crawled back through the opening she'd made, ecstatic that the worst was over.

"We got him, Sebastian," she said, praising her dog with the tone of her voice. "You did good."

She stood and began the perilous journey back across the floor, moving carefully, foot by foot, testing her weight with each step.

She contemplated a long plate of wood resting at an angle against the mound of broken tables she had to cross. There was no way around it. It looked sturdy enough, and she'd used it coming in, but when she took her first step onto the board—

Crack.

The plate gave out on her, flinging her onto her back. Had she not had Aaron in her arms, she might have been able to turn her body so she could land somewhat safely, or at least relatively painlessly, but as it was, she was all about protecting the little boy.

She hit a sharp pile of wreckage flat on her back, knocking the wind out of her, with her shoulder and hip taking the brunt force of the hit. For a moment she laid without moving, just staring at the ceiling and trying to reorient herself. She tried to roll sideways and back to her feet, but her body wasn't cooperating. Nothing moved. No matter how hard she concentrated, her legs simply wouldn't budge.

Everything was numb. The room was fading to pinpoints of black. At first she thought she'd broken her flashlight, but then she panicked when she realized the truth.

She was losing consciousness.

She had failed to save Aaron.

She took a deep, rasping breath. "Sebastian."

The dog whined and nosed her hand.

"Go find Eli. Find…"

And then the world went dark.

Eli was surprised to see Stephanie enter the church without Mary. She was wavering on her feet and clutching her belly. Eli grabbed a nearby wool blanket and wrapped it around her, urging her to sit.

"Where's Mary?" he asked the dazed woman.

She looked back at him with glassy eyes. "Preschool. Aaron."

Then she groaned and slumped forward. Eli wasn't sure, but he guessed Stephanie was in labor.

"Zach," he called to the medic across the room. "Lady with a baby over here."

Zach made a beeline for Stephanie, immediately assessing her and taking over caring for her needs. Delia was close behind, barking instructions for a cot to be emptied.

"Zach," he said, calling the medic aside. "Stephanie said something about a kid at the preschool. I think he might be hurt, and I'm pretty sure Mary went after him. Once you've got Stephanie stabilized, can you head that direction?"

Zach nodded, and Eli didn't wait for more. Something was going on with Mary, and he didn't know what. She'd left Stephanie to find her way over to the chapel on her own, while Mary went elsewhere. She wouldn't do that for no reason. It had to be something big.

Stephanie had mentioned the preschool, and presumably the name of one of her students.

Somehow Eli knew that was related to where Mary had gone, so he whistled for Bullet and took off down Main Street toward the preschool.

He was about halfway there when he was met by Sebastian. He'd never heard the dog bark so adamantly, nor had Sebastian ever acted so frantic. The Lab was generally a laid-back dog, but right now he had a wild look in his eyes, and Eli had to work to tamp down his phobia. It was only his fear that something had happened to Mary that kept him sane, especially when Sebastian grabbed the ankle of his pants and started pulling on him.

"What is it, boy? Did something happen to Mary?"

Once he'd said the words aloud, they became real. His heart burst in his chest as adrenaline coursed through him. His Mary was in trouble. Sebastian was trying to get his attention, not attack him.

"Show me, Sebastian. Where is Mary?"

He wasn't surprised when the dog turned and trotted toward the preschool, looking back every so often to make sure Eli was following.

When they reached the preschool, Eli was shocked to see what the storm had caused. His stomach turned when Sebastian crawled through a hole and into the building.

Mary was in there? Why would she go in alone? There was a major threat of a live electrical wire, to say nothing of the fallen debris.

To save a child.

Of course she would. Mary wouldn't think twice about plunging herself into danger if it meant saving someone's child.

Now it was up to Eli to save her.

"Are you ready, Bullet?"

The dog whined and followed Eli into the preschool.

"Search," he told Bullet. "Find Mary."

He shone his flashlight around the room, focusing on the left wing when Bullet plunged through a hole in the wreckage. Then he heard barking. Both dogs had made a hit.

Mary.

He ran toward the spot where Bullet had gone through. He growled in frustration. He was too big to fit in the hole. But when he aimed his light through, he could see the shadow of a person lying on her back, not moving, but cuddling a bundle in her arms.

With wild abandon, he started throwing debris aside—bricks, boards, school supplies. If it was in the way, it was gone. He had to get to his Mary, now. From what he could tell, she was unconscious, but she had little Aaron with her.

He didn't know what kind of shape he'd find either of them in, only that they weren't moving.

Not dead, he pleaded to God. *Please, don't let them be dead.*

When he'd made a hole half big enough for him to go through, he simply stepped back and rammed the rest of the way through with his shoulder, sprinted to Mary's side and dropped to his knees beside her and little Aaron.

"Oh, Lord. Oh, Lord," he kept praying, not caring that he was saying the words aloud, nor that he wasn't actually finishing his prayer. God knew everything in his heart, how much he loved Mary, and how he couldn't live without her.

"Mary, baby," he whispered, sweeping her hair back with his palm and leaning close enough to feel the slight brush of her breath on his cheek. "Come on, sweetheart. Wake up for me." He tucked Aaron into his arms and quickly examined him. He looked bruised, but his breath was strong. He appeared to be sleeping.

She had risked her own life to get this child to safety. Eli could do no less.

Boards creaked over his head. His pulse burned through him. He couldn't get both the boy and Mary out at once, but could he leave Mary when the roof might cave in?

He knew what she would want him to do. He swept his lips across her clammy forehead. "Aaron is safe, honey. You saved him. I'm coming back for you, baby. You're not alone. Bullet and Sebastian are here with you."

He commanded the dogs to stay, not that he needed to. They both understood Mary's dilemma. He crawled back through the opening he'd made in the wall as fast as he could with a child in his arms and without jeopardizing Aaron's safety, praying the whole time that the roof would hold until he could get back to Mary.

Just as he broke free of the door, he was surrounded by people, some from the chapel and others from the community center, where they'd pieced together what had happened. Someone had driven an ambulance over, and it was parked nearby, its lights flashing. In the center of the group, Phoebe, Aaron's mother, sobbed with relief as she reached for her child.

"Step back, everyone, and give them some room," Zach announced, helping Eli lower Aaron to the ground.

Eli grabbed Zach's shoulder. "Mary," was all he said.

Zach nodded. "Go, man."

Eli scrambled back into the preschool. His heart hammered as the roof made another frightening screech. He didn't have long—*they* didn't have long.

The dogs had both faithfully stayed by Mary's side. He was grateful she hadn't been alone, even for the short time he'd been gone.

She still hadn't moved, but at least her breath was stable. From what he could gather, the pile of debris she'd been crossing had given out on her. And in sheltering Aaron, she'd put herself at risk. He had no idea how badly she was hurt, but the fall had knocked her out. She could have a concussion or worse. No matter what, he had to get her out of there. There wasn't time or room to get a backboard for her. His arms would have to do.

As gently as he was able, he scooped her into his embrace and then gingerly stepped across the wreckage, determined not to fall as Mary had. He couldn't lose her. He just couldn't.

He ducked through the hole in the wall and breathed a sigh of relief. But he hadn't taken more than a few steps toward the front door before the rushing sound of the roof giving in thundered from behind him. He gasped, and broke into a dead run, both dogs at his side as he hovered his shoulders over Mary so she wouldn't be hit by any falling debris. A few pieces cut into him, but he barely felt them.

He was once more surrounded when he

broke free from the building. Zach was caring for Aaron inside the ambulance, and he knew Delia was back at the chapel shelter, but Ben Atwood and a couple of other men waited with a gurney to lay Mary upon.

"We'll take care of the two dogs," one of them said. "You go do what you have to do."

Eli never left her side as they strapped her in and rolled her to the ambulance. He was scared beyond belief that she hadn't yet gained consciousness. As he stepped into the ambulance with her, he prayed she soon would come back to him. And when she did, he would be right there, and he would never leave her again.

When Mary first opened her eyes, everything was blurry. She didn't know where she was, but after listening to the beeping, she realized she was in a hospital. She didn't remember what had happened. She only knew that her whole body ached.

She blinked rapidly, trying to work through the muddled details in her mind. She'd been in a building. There had been a lot of wreckage. There was a child.

"Aaron." The beep of her heart monitor raced. She'd passed out with the boy in her arms. Where was he? Was he safe?

A large, callused hand gripped hers.

"Aaron is fine, honey. They already released him from the hospital."

She breathed a sigh of relief. The boy was safe. They'd fallen and...

Her legs. She hadn't been able to move her legs.

She experienced a moment of sheer panic until she realized that she had, in fact, raised her knees when she'd become flustered. Apparently she still had use of her extremities.

She remembered feeling numb.

"What's wrong, honey?"

This time when Mary opened her eyes, her gaze was much sharper. Eli was hovering over her, worry evident in those expressive blue eyes. He looked bedraggled, as if he hadn't slept in a couple of days. Or shaved. His rough cheeks carried at least two days' growth of beard on them.

He was the most beautiful thing she'd ever seen. She wanted to reach up, wrap her arms around him and kiss him thoroughly.

How much pain medicine had they given her? She was positively loopy.

He smiled his quirky smile and brought her hand to his lips. "I can't say how glad I am to see you. Hey, I bought you some stuff."

He pointed to the table by her side.

Stuff? It looked like he'd emptied the entire

hospital gift shop. There was a huge bouquet of spring flowers in a gorgeous burgundy vase, an enormous brown teddy bear holding a heart-shaped box of chocolates and a half a dozen get-well balloons.

Her heart swelled until she thought she couldn't bear it any longer. Eli had done all that for her? She chuckled, not even caring if it hurt.

"What? Is it too cliché?"

"It's too much! These are all from you?" she exclaimed.

"Yeah." He rubbed the back of his neck. "Everything on that table, anyway. I guess it is a bit of overkill."

He was still holding her hand, and she enveloped it in both of hers. "No. That's not what I meant at all. I can't believe you've done so much for me."

"He hasn't left the room since you got here," came Alexis's voice from the far side of the room.

"Alexis?" Mary tried to sit up, but slumped right back down again. Every single muscle in her body must be bruised.

"Don't go trying to move, silly," Alexis said, coming to the other side of the bed and laying a hand on her shoulder. "Samantha was here, too, and she sends her love. She had to go back to her shift at the store."

"Thank her for me when you see her."

"I will. I've got to run, too, now. I was just here to see how you were doing and if Eli needed anything. I'm glad you're awake. I know Eli will take good care of you. And the doctors," she said, as if it were an afterthought.

Mary turned back to Eli. "Is it true you haven't left the hospital? How long has it been?"

"Two days," a female voice she didn't recognize said from the door. "He hasn't even left your room, except when you're being examined. Now that's devotion for you."

Eli's sister, Vee, stepped into Mary's sight range and offered a small bouquet of carnations. "I can't compete with my brother," she said with a laugh.

"No. These are beautiful."

"He saved you, too, you know. He and Bullet."

Could her heart grow any bigger? What she felt for him defied words. Eli was her hero, now and always.

"See? I knew you could do it," she whispered to him. "As far as I'm concerned, you've passed your final exam. You and Bullet are a bona fide K-9 unit."

"Considering Eli's issues, I'm giving you *both* gold stars. Ben is waiting for me downstairs. I just wanted to say hi and that the family loves you."

"Thank you," she called, but Vee was already out the door. What did Vee mean about the family loving her? They didn't even know her that well. And what was that about Eli's issues?

"What did she mean?" She didn't press any further than that. Eli could explain, or not explain, as he saw fit.

He perched on the side of the bed and laid his arm across the blanket around her waist. "I should have told you a long time ago."

"Told me what?"

"About me and…" He hesitated. "Dogs."

She had no idea what he was talking about, but his expression was as serious as she'd ever seen it. "Go on."

"When I was little, I was attacked by a wolf hybrid."

"Oh, Eli."

"It left scars. Inside and out. Mostly inside. I never really got over it."

"You mean…?"

"I'm terrified of dogs."

Mary had a hard time believing Eli was afraid of anything, but fears weren't always rational, and his certainly had a basis in reality.

"Then why…?"

"Why did I sign up for the K-9 unit? I didn't,

really. I kind of got forced into it. I just didn't argue against it when the captain told me I'd been selected. After that bad break with Natalie, I was fighting for my reputation. I thought the K-9 thing would help. I know I was a pretty big jerk to you when we first started."

"I only wish I had known." She didn't know how she would have worked to help him deal with his phobia, but she could have done something. And it certainly explained a lot.

He sighed. "It is what it is. And I'm getting better."

"You have Bullet living at your house!" She was astounded that he could have faced his fear head-on like that.

"I know, right?" He laughed. "And the funniest thing is, I'm kind of used to him now. I can't imagine coming home to my apartment without him."

"Alexis's ranch has a lot of room for him to run."

His brow furrowed. "Redemption Ranch? What does that have to do with anything?"

She bit the inside of her lip until her emotions were under control. She loved Eli. More than anything, she wanted him to be happy.

"You don't have to hide anything from me. I know how you feel about Alexis. I've seen the two of you together."

"You know how I feel about…*Alexis?*"

She tried to smile. She really did. "She's a wonderful woman. Maybe I'm jumping the gun a little bit, but she'll make a great wife."

His gaze widened and then one side of his lips crept up. "I'm sure she will."

Mary let out her breath. It was settled, then. She should feel relieved. Instead she felt like there were millions of little springs all wound up inside her.

"Yeah, honey, but not *my* wife."

"I'm sorry. What?" She couldn't have heard him correctly.

"I'll admit I've been spending a lot of time with Alexis."

She nodded.

"But she was trying to figure out how to set me up with *you.*"

"I… You…" she stammered. Her heart started racing, but her mind and emotions simply couldn't keep up.

"That's right, honey. Me and you. It's been you all the time."

"But I thought—"

"Wrong. Clearly, communicating isn't one of my fine points. You didn't need to have a building fall on you to get my attention," he teased, his eyes twinkling and that beautiful smile beaming just for her. "I've loved you all along."

She was gaping. She knew she was gaping. She couldn't seem to get her jaw to work. He had risked his own life to save her—because he *loved* her.

And, oh, how she loved him.

He leaned forward until his lips were inches away, his warm breath mingling with hers. "I think this is the part where you say you love me, too," he suggested with a low rumble that came from deep in his throat.

"I love you, too."

"Now, that wasn't so hard, was it?"

Never, ever would she have expected to be in Eli's arms, in his *heart*. But that's what he'd said. That's what the gleam in his eyes repeated. And the curve of his smile as he leaned even closer.

"This part's not so complicated, either," he whispered, before he covered her lips with his own, sealing their hearts together.

Epilogue

Four Months Later

"Is she coming?" Eli was more than a little bit antsy. He'd been at Redemption Ranch since sunup, decorating Alexis's house for Mary's surprise birthday party. He wanted to oversee every detail. It all had to be perfect.

"Relax, Eli," Alexis said with a laugh. "She's on her way. Samantha's got her covered."

"And she doesn't suspect anything?"

"Not a chance. If she did, she would have told Samantha or me. Take a breath before you hyperventilate."

"I'm terrified that I'm going to mess this up."

Alexis stopped taping curled purple crepe paper to the wall and rolled her eyes at Eli. "There is no possible way you can mess this up. With what you've got planned, none of the rest of it matters." She grinned at him. "However, you might want to put Bullet out back until she gets here. If she sees him, you'll be made."

"Oh, right." As he went out front to get Bullet, he greeted all of Mary's many friends who were arriving for the party. As far as they knew, it was just a surprise birthday bash. As far as Mary knew, she was helping out with Alexis's teenage intake process again.

He whistled for his dog and two more came running. He assumed they belonged to Alexis. He'd been working with a counselor, and now he felt no more than a twinge when a strange dog ran up to him. The twinge would probably never go away completely, but he could live with it. If it was the price he had to pay to have Mary in his life, then he'd even embrace it. He put Bullet in the field behind the house and hurried back in so he wouldn't miss Mary's arrival.

"She's here," Alexis announced, hushing everybody and waving the sound down with her hands. She flipped off the lights, and they all crouched down, waiting for the big moment.

Eli's heart was beating so hard he could hear it in his ears, and it wasn't just because he was about to surprise Mary. Or at least, it wasn't about the birthday party.

"Where's Alexis?" he heard Mary ask from the porch. "It doesn't even look like anybody's home."

"She's probably inside," Samantha assured her, turning the knob and stepping back.

Alexis flipped the switch and the room was flooded with light.

"Surprise!" everyone called, then rushed forward to give Mary hugs and well wishes. Eli leaned his shoulder against the wall and crossed his arms, enjoying the attention the love of his life was getting.

She didn't know how special she was. It was his lifetime mission to remind her, every single day, in every way he could think of.

Today, it was a surprise party.

"It appears you have lots of friends," he said when he finally saw an opening and moved to her side. He pressed a quick kiss to her lips, enjoying the way she colored. He loved that he could make her blush.

But now there were tears in her eyes.

"What's the matter, honey? I thought you'd be happy about this."

"I am," she assured him. "It's just that...I didn't know I had so many people who cared for me."

"Well, you do. Me, most of all."

She caressed his cheek and his heart glowed. "I know."

"I'd better go get Bullet," he said. "I locked him out back so you wouldn't see him when you came in." That he had secondary motives for leaving her side was left unsaid.

He did get Bullet, but he also took a detour through Alexis's den to pick up something else.

When he reached the living room, he nodded to Alexis. He couldn't breathe, and he felt like someone had tied his stomach in knots, but it was time.

"Attention, everyone," she called, and the room quieted. "Mary, front and center, birthday girl."

He caught her eye as she stepped forward, and winked at her. She beamed back at him. He loved her smile. He loved everything about her.

"Present time, present time, open your present, see what's inside!" Alexis chimed.

Mary raised her eyebrows. "Well, I would, but I don't see a present."

That was his cue. He put his fluffy little bundle on the floor and nudged her forward.

Mary gasped in surprise. "A Saint Bernard? For me?"

Eli stepped forward. "Of course it's for you, sweetheart. You said you wanted one of these things, although looking at her paws, I'm guessing I may live to regret this. She's going to get huge."

Mary laughed and scooped the puppy off the floor, cuddling it under her chin.

"I figured I have a dog, and you have dogs, plural—but *we* don't have one."

Tears formed in the corner of her beautiful green eyes. "I don't… Are you…" she stammered.

Alexis cut in. "I said, open the present, see what's inside."

"But she's a dog," Mary protested. "How do I—"

Her sentence came to an abrupt halt as she noticed the jewelry box tied to the puppy's collar, almost like one of those barrels the adult Saint Bernards sometimes wore.

His heart in his throat, Eli stepped forward and untied the box, and then, in front of God and all of their friends, he dropped to one knee.

"Mary Travis, I've given you every kind of grief there is, and you put up with it all. I've never met a woman I've admired more. Your tenderness, your sensitivity and most of all your love. I would be honored if you would agree to become my wife."

She only hesitated for the second it took to shift the puppy from her left arm to her right. Then she offered him her hand, her heart and her life.

* * * * *

Dear Reader,

Welcome back to Serendipity, Texas, where the second of the Little Chicks, Mary Travis, finally has the opportunity to meet her match.

Eli Bishop is a strong man with a solid faith in God, but after he faces some tough obstacles in his life experiences, he's shaken and confused. At those moments when he believes everything has fallen apart, God is actually leading him in a different—and better—direction.

Sometimes our own life experiences give us tunnel vision, but our Lord sees the big picture. Even during our most difficult moments, God is there with us, guiding us even when we have no idea where to go. In Him we have a hope and a future.

I hope you enjoyed *Her Valentine Sheriff*. I love to connect with you, my readers, in a personal way. Please look me up at my website, www.debkastnerbooks.com. You can find my Facebook page at www.facebook.com/debkastnerbooks, or catch me on Twitter @debkastner.

Please know that you are daily in my prayers.

Love Courageously,

Deb Kastner

Questions for Discussion

1. Eli sometimes acted curt or unreasonable with Mary, but his motives were sincere. In truth, he reacted out of deep need. Consider a time in your own life where someone acted in a way you didn't understand. Did you find out their motives later, and were they different than you expected? How did you react?

2. In what ways can we respond charitably when those with whom we associate don't speak or act as we believe they should?

3. Eli is worried that he and Mary have too many differences to be a successful couple, yet Frank and Jo contrast each other and still share an abiding love. Do opposites attract? And can true love result?

4. Looking back on his life, Eli believes that sometimes God has to strong-arm him into making right decisions. Can you remember a time in your own life where God took the reins to guide you into a better situation?

5. Eli is close to his family and wants to be a family man himself. Do you think that it

was indicative of his poor relationship with Natalie that he never spent time with her family?

6. Which character was your favorite, or to which one did you most relate? Why?

7. What do you do when God says no to something you thought was right for you? Are life's disappointments always a bad thing?

8. Eli refused to tell anyone the truth about his phobia. Why do you think it was so important to him that others not know?

9. Sometimes our best is not God's best. Read Jeremiah 29:11 and discuss how it relates to your own life.

10. Eli is stunned to realize that God not only uses his strengths to help people but also his weaknesses and vulnerabilities. Share how this rings true in your life.

11. Compare and contrast Mary and Natalie. Why do you think they are so different?

12. Mary has always felt like she hides behind her two more outgoing best friends, yet she is included in the town moniker the Little

Chicks. Do you think folks in Serendipity see her as she sees herself?

13. Mary misreads the situation between Alexis and Eli. Sometimes what appears obvious is not what it seems. Have you ever experienced a situation where your perceptions were off, or someone made incorrect assumptions about you? How did you feel?

14. Why was Mary so self-conscious when Eli carried her back to her vehicle after she sprained her ankle? What makes you feel uncomfortable?

15. Is there a moral to this story? If so, what is it?

LARGER-PRINT BOOKS!

GET 2 FREE LARGER-PRINT NOVELS PLUS 2 FREE MYSTERY GIFTS

Love Inspired

Larger-print novels are now available...

LILPDIR13R